CW00606977

989900422279 99

The Shadow of Iron Eyes

Blinded after an accident the infamous bounty hunter known as Iron Eyes roams south aimlessly hoping his sight might return when his instinct leads him to the scene of brutal murder. Flames lick the sky as bodies burn within the confines of a small cattle ranch. As Iron Eyes dismounts and tries to learn more, he hears and feels rifle fire. Wounded, he falls, and then lies helpless as someone attempts to finish the job.

What happens next leads the injured bounty hunter further south to a place where only the Devil would feel at home. A place where the law has never ventured, a place where Iron Eyes will kill anyone who stands in his way.

The Shadow of Iron Eyes

Rory Black

A Black Horse Western

ROBERT HALE · LONDON

© Rory Black 2011
First published in Great Britain 2011

ISBN 978-0-7090-9247-6

Robert Hale Limited
Clerkenwell House
Clerkenwell Green
London EC1R 0HT

www.halebooks.com

Typeset by
Derek Doyle & Associates, Shaw Heath
Printed and bound in Great Britain by
CPI Antony Rowe, Chippenham and Eastbourne

PROLOGUE

Mason Burr was a large bulky man. He had never done an honest day's work in his entire thirty-five years of life and yet he was wealthy. Some men instinctively know how to make money and he was one of them. He knew how to trick even the most cautious of his fellow men out of their life savings. There were no depths to which Burr would not sink to get his hands on other people's hard-earned savings, and that had always included killing. Burr had always managed to keep what other men called scruples at arm's length; they never interfered with his ultimate goals.

Burr was unlike most wanted men, though, and had always travelled alone. He had never required the help of anyone else in order to achieve his objectives.

He had a mind like a sidewinder. Always ready to twist and turn and strike out to kill anyone who got

5

in his way. No one ever managed to get too close. He had honed his appearance over the years until he resembled a banker rather than what he truly was. By all the yardsticks by which most of us measure others Burr was the most honest-looking man anyone had ever set eyes upon. Like most real bankers, though, Burr could never quite get enough money to bathe and wallow in.

His life had become a deadly game. He could have retired years earlier and lived handsomely off the spoils of his devilish occupation but, like a compulsive gambler, he always had to play one more hand. Nothing could equal the pleasure Burr managed to get from leaving others destitute and then ultimately dead. He had lost count of how many victims there were littered behind the tails of his frock-coat. But Burr never looked backwards. He always aimed his eyes forward towards the next sucker.

His bulk was always well disguised beneath the most expensive of tailored attire and his personal grooming never did anything but add to the image he had crafted for himself. Well-spoken and seemingly generous, the outlaw had only once come close to having a noose tightened around his neck. That had been five years earlier when he had misjudged the intelligence of those who knew his innocent victim. Yet even a jailhouse could not hold Burr. He had managed to trick his way free and flee south to the less lawful Texas. There he had remained to continue his ruthless pursuit of obtaining other people's money and then killing them.

During his five years' travelling around the vast state he had accumulated another fortune which dwarfed his previous one. A fortune which was spread out in more banks than most other outlaws could have dreamed existed. Bad money became good money.

In all his days there had been just one chink in his otherwise impenetrable suit of armour. For when he had fallen into the hands of the law they had taken photographic images of him. The only actual weakness in his life was that crude but accurate pictures existed of his distinctive face. They had adorned Wanted posters and Burr knew only too well that one day one of those old posters would pop up to betray him.

For all his skill at being the depraved but cunning creature he actually was Burr knew that having had his image captured whilst he awaited hanging was a mistake. A mistake which he could never rectify.

One day someone would put the man and the image together and know who they were actually dealing with. The spectre of death would return with its hefty price tag as a sweetener to those who made their living by hunting those the law had forgotten about.

There was one thing which Texas had in abundance and that was bounty hunters. With the law thin on the ground the strange breed of men who lived their lives by capturing and killing wanted outlaws were always busy.

Always somewhere close.

He had seen a hundred of them since he had arrived in the lone star state but so far none of them had given the respectable-looking Burr a second glance. One day that would alter. One day one of them would have one of those ancient Wanted posters in his possession and would recognize him. As surely as leaves drop from trees in the fall, that day would inevitably arrive.

For that very reason, Burr had never remained too long in any town or city, for fear of being recognized by someone. Someone who could not be sweet-talked. Someone who would kill because the Wanted poster allowed it.

Dead or alive.

No bounty hunter worth his salt could or would turn his back on that proclamation. Burr knew bounty hunters seldom took the second option. Prisoners were always dangerous. Corpses never offered anything but a feast for flies and then a hand-some, if bloody, pay-day.

For all his wealth and deadly cunning his fear became unusually oppressive while he was in the small border town known as Rio Bravos on a hot, humid Saturday evening in one of its numerous can-tinas. The sun had set an hour earlier and a string of

8

coal-oil lanterns glowed across the sprawling settlement. Their light not only attracted countless moths but other, two-legged, creatures who sought the illumination of their prey.

Burr had been in Rio Bravos for fewer than three days. He was resting after managing not only to sell a gold-mine that did not exist but then, after pocketing the $1,000 in gold coin, contriving to kill his victim in what everyone had described as a terrible accident.

The sound of guitars had led Burr to the cantina. The room was long, the atmosphere aromatic. Most of those inside were at the far end close to the hot ovens. Burr had seated himself opposite the entrance, where a drape of beaded strings swayed in the gentle evening air keeping the moths and hungry flies at bay. The bowl of chilli seemed to be more alive than usual but Burr, for all his stylish outward appearance, would eat almost anything placed before him. A childhood of near starvation had taught the outlaw never to refuse food, however obnoxious it might appear.

Burr tore off a chunk of still-warm bread, dipped it into the dark-brown meat and was about to put it into his mouth when he noticed the broad-shouldered man standing just beyond the moving curtain of colourful beads. An oil lantern perched on a wall just outside the cantina entrance illuminated one side of the strange-looking man, who held a cigar firmly gripped between his teeth.

As always Burr was alert to any possible danger. He lowered his free left hand from the table as the fingers of his right continued to dip the bread into the aromatic food. He found one of his guns, which were well hidden by the expert tailoring of his long frock-coat, and eased it from its customized holster set, like its twin, on his hip.

The sound of guitars being played at the end of the long cantina masked the sound of the gun hammer as his thumb eased it back on the gait until it locked into position.

Burr moved the weapon from under the silk-lined skirt of his coat and rested it beneath the table on his left thigh. Its five-inch barrel was aimed at the swaying beaded curtain and the figure who stood behind it.

With narrowed eyes Burr watched as the man ran a match down the wall beneath the lantern. A flame erupted and was sucked into the length of the cigar. Smoke billowed around the man's head as he shook the match and dropped it.

Who was he?

The question burned into Burr's mind.

A hungry man would already have entered. This man just stared at him as he sat in the well-lit cantina.

In the three days he had been in Rio Bravos the elegant outlaw had not set eyes upon this man. Burr concentrated and focused hard on what he could see of the man behind the moving lines of beads.

He was taller than average. Certainly not Mexican. Burr had never seen a Mexican who looked like that, Burr told himself. He wore a trail coat that still carried the dust of a long ride. It also carried the evidence of countless kills. As the curtain-beads moved Burr caught sight of gun grips jutting from the man's belt. They glinted in the light of the lantern as the man sucked on his cigar and remained rooted to the spot as though considering whether to enter or not.

A trace of sweat trickled down from the well-groomed hair of the seated man. Burr took a bite of the chilli-soaked bread and chewed as he kept watching the stranger.

The tall stranger was obviously looking at him with more than a hint of recognition carved into his face. The elegant outlaw thought about the Wanted posters again. That damned photgraph which, unlike so many others, looked like the person it was meant to represent.

Burr had lost his appetite but knew he could do nothing but remain at the table. To move now might be the last thing he ever did. Every sinew in the outlaw's body was screaming at him.

Bounty hunter.

The man inhaled on the long black cigar again. This time the scarlet light from its burning tip lit up the face of the stranger.

Burr could see his eyes.

11

His cold hollow eyes.

Eyes which were aimed straight at him.

Bounty hunter.

There was nothing else this creature could possibly be, he kept telling himself. At last, after five years, one of them had caught up with him. What had he done wrong? Had his last victim pointed a dying finger after him?

Wanted dead or alive.

For a reward of $2,000.

Dead or alive.

Mason Burr swallowed hard. He curled his index finger around the trigger of his cocked .44 and inhaled deeply. He had to be ready. Ready to kill this man if he was what he suspected. It had been many years since he had killed anyone face on. Most of his victims had not seen the deadly gun when he had discharged its lethal fury. Burr felt sweat rolling unchecked down his spine beneath his immaculate clothing.

A thin-fingered hand parted the beads and the tall man stepped into the cantina. No nightmare could have even come close to what this tall man looked like. Death was carved into every inch of the lean figure. Dried blood stained the tails of his long trail coat.

His eyes burned across the room at Burr.

The guitars stopped playing.

Slowly one of the thin bony hands reached into a

12

pocket and pulled out a folded sheet of paper. The man shook it until it opened up. Cigar smoke drifted up into eyes which darted from the Wanted poster to the seated man with the bowl of chilli before him. Then he rammed the paper back into his coat pocket and took one step forward.

There was a hushed silence in the cantina.

'Ya sure took some finding,' the bounty hunter said.

Burr watched the bounty hunter's fingers flex above his gun-grips.

'You must be mistaking me for some other *hombre.*'

'Dead or alive means only one thing in my book, Burr,' the bounty hunter whispered in deathly tones. Tones which only his target could hear.

Mason Burr held on to his gun hidden beneath the table and leaned back in his chair. 'Is that so?'

'Yep,' the chilling voice answered. 'It means ya dead.'

Burr nodded as though accepting his fate. A fate he had willingly dished out to countless innocent people over the preceding years but one that he was reluctant to countenance for himself. 'Reckon you can draw them hoglegs fast enough to kill a man who has a .44 aimed at ya guts?'

The smile was twisted. 'Yep. Like I said, ya already dead but ya ain't smart enough to know it yet.'

The outlaw did not bother to respond to the jibe. Suddenly without warning Burr raised both legs and kicked the table away from his chair. It careered into the bounty hunter a fraction of a heartbeat after Burr had seen the man's thin hands drag both guns from his belt. Gunsmoke encircled the deafening white-hot shafts of rage that blasted from the well-dressed outlaw's gun as he fanned its hammer.

The wounded bounty hunter staggered but managed to unleash lead from his own drawn weapons. Roaring fury exploded in both directions, lethal lead flashed back and forth as both men blasted their weaponry.

The entire exchange lasted a mere twenty seconds.

Acrid black smoke hung on the stale air of the cantina, masking both men for another few moments. Then the breeze blowing in from the street dispersed the fug to reveal the bloody outcome of the duel.

The screams of females at the far end of the long room filled Burr's ears as he managed to rise from his chair and stare at the body stretched out before him. Smoke still rose from the barrels of both guns in the bounty hunter's lifeless hands.

Screwing up his eyes against the burning smoke, Burr brushed himself down to reassure himself that he was remarkably uninjured. He glanced over his shoulder at the whitewashed wall behind him. It bore the holes of every one of the bounty hunter's bullets. Burr shook the hot casings from his gun and

14

reloaded the .44 with fresh bullets from the belt of his hidden holster.

Like moths drawn to a naked flame all of the people who had been inside the cantina gathered around the still-immaculate outlaw. Burr knelt and pulled the incriminating poster from the man's pocket and hurriedly crushed it into one of his own. He did not want any of the startled witnesses to know the truth.

'Who was he, *señor*?' a man in a sombrero asked fearfully.

'Probably an outlaw.' Burr turned the body over. He had placed five bullets into the bounty hunter's heart. A mere two inches separated the grouping of bullet holes in the chest of the dead man. He then found a well-thumbed envelope and stared at the name upon it. The name of Jackson Smith meant nothing to Burr but he pocketed that as well. Again he feared the law's realizing that the dead man was indeed a bounty hunter. 'Reckon he must have thought he'd found an easy target. I sure was lucky.'

The beaded curtain parted again. Every eye went to the man with a tin star pinned to his vest as he rushed in with a Winchester clutched in his gloved hands.

'What happened here?'

The people all pointed at the body and the pool of blood which had already spread around it.

'He come in looking to kill,' one man drawled.

'An outlaw tried to kill Señor Burr, Sheriff,' one of the other voices said.

'Mr Burr just defended himself,' a female added.

The lawman patted Burr's shoulder. 'Ya a mighty lucky man, Mr Burr. These stinking outlaws come up over the border and kill just for fun of it. Good job ya had a gun to protect yaself with. Anybody know who this critter was?'

There was no response. Burr gave a sigh of relief.

'What ya doing in Rio Bravos, Mr Burr?' the sheriff asked casually as he kicked the boot of the dead man lying on the floor.

'Business,' Burr replied.

'Yep. Ya was mighty lucky.'

Slyly Mason Burr nodded. 'Reckon so.'

16

ONE

There was nothing but silence all through the forest as the morning sun blazed high above the canopy of trees, vainly attempting to penetrate the dense foliage. Not one of the millions of living things that inhabited the woodland dared to make a sound. Every eye of every creature watched the silent intruder who allowed his mount to find its own route through the trees. For they instinctively sensed who it was that sat astride the tall palomino stallion.

It was the angel of death.

The most ruthless of hunters.

Iron Eyes.

The sickening scent of a lifetime of kills hung to every part of the horseman. Its nauseating aroma moved ahead of the apparently lifeless rider as though warning everything in his path to be aware that soon they might be added to his incalculable tally. Yet Iron Eyes was not mindful of anything as he hung over the saddle horn and allowed the powerful mount to find its own way around yet another hindrance placed before them by unseen gods or demons. To the unperceptive he might have seemed dead. There was no movement in the frail emaciated form as it balanced in the well-sculptured Mexican saddle. No hint of the deadly danger for which he was infamous.

There was no thrusting of the vicious bloodstained spurs.

Nothing to suggest that life still existed in the pitiful bounty hunter. He simply slumped like a rag doll and allowed his horse to venture on. Only his long black hair had any animation in its matted tresses.

A dead man might have seemed more alive.

Those who had run into the bounty hunter before this moment would not have recognized him at first. The previous few months had taken a hefty toll on the already battle-scarred figure. The addition of a strange skull cap crafted out of cement would only have added to the confusion. For only a couple of people knew that Iron Eyes's skull had been shattered during a saloon brawl. A small town sawbones had saved the bounty hunter's life by wrapping bandages tightly around the fractured bones and then covering them in cement.

It had been a crude but effective way to stop the skull's segments from moving until they had a chance of healing, yet there had been a problem.

A real big problem for a man who existed by hunting down those with reward money on their heads.

It had left him blind.

On occasion his sight had returned briefly, but then the darkness came back to torment him.

How could a bounty hunter exist if he could not see the images on the Wanted posters buried deep in his pockets? How could he know who he was facing?

Know who to kill?

Iron Eyes had never lost any shuteye by killing anyone who had got in his way but that had been before the last showdown, Before the blackness had blanketed his every waking moment.

Only two men actually knew of his plight. The sawbones, and a sheriff who had helped him. All others who had encountered Iron Eyes since his accident had not realized that the deadly bounty hunter was unable to see anything. He had managed to hide his disability from all onlookers with a courageous mixture of bravado and the use of his other heightened senses.

Yet that had proved taxing.

It required total concentration.

After a short while Iron Eyes had realized that his luck would run out sooner rather than later if he kept up his pretence. He had stocked up on a generous supply of cigars, whiskey and jerky for himself and oats for his most precious possession, his newly acquired stallion. Then in the dead of night he had taken to the trail again.

For months the bounty hunter had kept away from humanity and allowed his horse to guide him. The palomino was strong. Far stronger than all the other horses the rider had used over the years. Unlike the numerous Indian ponies his owner had once favoured, this creature had the strength to outrun anything they had yet encountered.

Iron Eyes trusted the horse more than he had ever trusted any other living thing. He trusted it to find water every day. Never take them into danger. Always to be sure-footed and never to stumble and dislodge its master.

It had become his eyes.

Iron Eyes knew that he must keep riding on and on. He was searching for something he felt was out there, somewhere waiting to be discovered. The place where his eyes would start to work again. The place where his sight would return permanently and allow him to resume his deadly career.

Allow him to see those he hunted and kill them.

Iron Eyes knew that it was a long shot. Maybe a vain hope, but it was all he had left. A man needs something to aim his guns at even if it be only a target set deep in his tired thoughts.

He reined in and inhaled deeply. There was a smell in the forest that he had never noticed before.

20

A freshness that sighted folks never recognized. The stallion snorted as though grateful for a moment's rest. Iron Eyes lifted his head and stared with unseeing eyes all around them. He could hear nothing except the breeze that whistled through the trees that surrounded both horse and rider.

There was no danger here, he told himself.

No reason for him to claw his matched pair of Navy Colts from his belt and start shooting. The stallion had again guided them to another safe haven.

Iron Eyes carefully looped his leg over the neck of the horse and slid to the ground. It was a well practised manoeuvre which had fooled a lot of people before he had set out on his quest. He opened the nearer of his satchels, pulled out a bottle of whiskey and tugged its cork free with his teeth. He took a long swig then replaced the cork and returned the bottle to the saddle-bags. The sound of glass bottles clinking one against another reassured him that he still had enough provisions to last a few more days.

Last him until he reached another town.

He could hear the stallion munching as it wandered, grazing over the grass. The thin figure pulled a twisted cigar from his pocket and placed it in the corner of his mouth. He struck a match with his thumbnail, cupped its flame and inhaled long and deep.

'Where the hell are we, horse?' Iron Eyes asked his mount as smoke drifted through his teeth.

21

TWO

The morning air was fresh and yet the merciless sun was already drying the ground which surrounded the ranch house and its high-roofed barn. The bleached poles which marked out the various sections of the small cattle ranch were crude, but fit for purpose. The herd of white-faced cattle were penned in from all sides. A stream ran down from the forested hillside behind the small homestead and right through the heart of the paddock where the animals grazed.

It was exactly like so many other ranches. Hard work had built this out of the wilderness close to the border. Sweat and a good dose of faith had created something which was about to start repaying those who had slaved for so many years.

Yet the man and his woman and their offspring would never taste the fruits of their combined labours. Never be able to turn their sweat into cash.

There were others who had already decided to do

22

that for them. Others who had ridden across the border during the warm star-filled night until they had reached the place that they intended to raise to the ground. Others with only one thing on their minds: to do whatever it took to take everything, brutally, from these poor people.

Dust drifted from the hoofs of their lathered-up mounts.

There were seven of them. Each man was armed with more weaponry than any innocent drifter might require to travel through this landscape. The men wore a mix of Stetsons and sombreros. Each man was wanted for more crimes than any Wanted poster might be able to list on its single sheet of paper. Like so many of their breed they feared nothing except one another.

The self-appointed leader of the devilish group was known as Mexican Pete. He was an outlaw who had killed his first man at the age of twelve simply because he wanted to. There was a look about the wanted man who sloped over the horn of his saddle which put the fear of death into all whom he encountered. A deep scar curled down his face between his eyes from sombrero to chin. Stained teeth smiled at the sight before them as he sucked on a cigar. He had already sold the cattle he stared down at. Now all he had to do was rustle and deliver them.

Kansas-born Ty Harper had ridden beside Pete for more than five years, until now they had started to be able to read each other's thoughts. He edged his pinto close to the grinning outlaw leader and nodded as if he had just heard Mexican Pete saying something.

The five others were the scum they had managed to accumulate on the long ride north. Men who did others' bidding for a share of the profit their hideous actions always brought them. Apart from a skilled back-shooter known only as Pedro the others were simply hired help.

'When we going to ride in?' Pedro asked anxiously.

The cruel eyes of Pete glanced at the five riders beside Harper. He then spat a lump of black goo over the head of his mount. 'How many folks you see?'

None of the five others next to Harper had an answer.

Mexican Pete sighed. 'Tell them, Ty.'

Harper rubbed his chin. 'I counted five.'

Pete gave a slow smiling nod. '*Sí.* Five.'

'A man and his bitch and three young'uns,' Ty Harper added.

'Hardsome bitch,' Mexican Pete drooled. 'I shall enjoy her before slitting her throat.'

'Reckon we can have us a little fun after we kill all the others?' a curious Pedro wondered aloud before rubbing his groin. 'I got me an itch that needs tending.'

'Maybe,' Pete replied.

The five horsemen beside Harper all looked disgruntled by Mexican Pete's vague reply.

'What if we have the kids, *amigo*?' a bandit named One-eared Sanchez asked. 'I like the little ones.'

Harper gave a slow nod. 'As long as we kill that rancher ya can have whatever ya likes, One-ear.'

'I think One-ear is happy now.' Pete nodded.

The riders gathered up their reins and readied themselves.

'How many steers can ya see?' Harper asked them.

'Many.' One of the other sombrero wearing outlaws nodded as if his answer was accurate.

After tossing his cigar away, Mexican Pete drew one of his long barrelled six-shooters and kissed it fondly. 'I am ready. Let's go have us some fun.'

The riders spurred. As their horses galloped down the hillside towards the unsuspecting ranch and its innocent occupants they started to unleash their arsenal.

Blazing tapers of lethal venom cut through the dry air as the wide-eyed horses beneath them closed in on their prey. Within a matter of seconds the rancher had been caught in the deathly crossfire. The shooting continued.

THREE

Smouldering remnants of what had once been a sturdy ranch house adjoined by a barn was all that remained on the blackened land where once hundreds of white-faced steers had grazed. Stubborn flames flickered as they gnawed on the last of the buildings' lumber. The acrid stench of kerosene lingered on the morning air as declaration that this had not been anything but deliberate arson. The revolting smell of burning flesh haunted the entire area as it too drifted on the black twisting spirals of rising smoke. The land just north of the border to Mexico had always been dangerous but it had never been subjected to anything like this.

Every inch of the ground was scarred by the hoof-marks of the riders who had rustled and killed to get their hands on what they craved. Yet the horseman who steered his tall palomino stallion down the forested slope towards the scene of destruction could

26

see none of this.

For the first time for weeks Iron Eyes had taken hold of his reins and curiously guided his mount toward the stench that others would have avoided like the plague. He had been drawn here by the scent of death.

A familiar scent which filled his flared nostrils and painted lurid images in his mind. Images that his eyes could not perceive.

The mighty horse beneath him shied and attempted to pull away from where its master was forcing it to keep heading. Iron Eyes stood in his stirrups and balanced as his honed senses tried to explain what he was approaching.

The emaciated bounty hunter eased back on the reins of the powerful animal beneath him. The stallion stopped. Iron Eyes looped his long leathers around the saddle horn and slowly lowered himself back down upon his saddle.

Like a trusty gun-hound Iron Eyes sniffed the air which surrounded him. It told him a story his eyes had seen many times before. He knew exactly what had occurred. It was there, painted in vivid colour.

The putrid aroma of the burning bodies only added to the sad picture which was filling his thoughts.

Although he had mercilessly dispatched many wanted outlaws in his time even Iron Eyes could not stomach the thought of mindless slaughter. It went against the brutal image which had grown around the infamous bounty hunter over the years but Iron Eyes had never actually killed anyone who was innocent.

He was not about to start now. Not knowingly, anyway.

The nervous stallion gave out a complaining snort. Like its master it did not like the smell which surrounded them on the morning breeze. Iron Eyes listened to the animal as it clawed at the dry ground with its hoof.

'Easy,' the bounty hunter drawled.

There had been a time months earlier when Iron Eyes had actually believed the doctor who had patched him up. Believed he would regain his sight, but, as weeks had lengthened into months he had grown to accept that his once keen eyesight was gone.

Gone for ever.

Iron Eyes sniffed at the air again.

He tried to detect where the water on this unknown land might be. The mighty stallion needed a drink. His alert senses told him that there was either a well or a trough, or even a waterhole somewhere within the confines of this place.

Nobody could raise cattle on land which had no water.

Since becoming the owner of the proud palomino, after killing its *vaquero* master a year earlier, the bounty hunter had tried to ensure it never went thirsty or hungry.

The stallion had saved his bacon on more than one occasion. He owed this animal a debt.

Iron Eyes always honoured his debts. All the other small Indian ponies had been little more than creatures that he rode and spurred until they dropped, but this huge horse was different. He had never liked horses but this one promised the difference between life and death.

Iron Eyes tilted his head away from the source of the smoke to his left and then caught the familiar fragrance. His long thin fingers pulled the reins to turn the horse's head, then he tapped his spurs.

The stallion began to walk across the uneven ground to where a trough filled with water stood beside a much-used pump. He felt the stallion's head drop and listened to it drinking its fill as he carefully looped his leg over his saddle horn and slid to the dusty ground.

Blindness was bad for a man who had earned his living by hunting both animal and human alike throughout his entire adult life. Without eyes that worked he had not been able to study reward posters. Had not been able to know who was wanted and what they looked like. His Navy Colts had become almost redundant.

Yet losing his sight had honed all his other senses until they were razor sharp. He had not noticed it at first, but then it began to dawn upon him. He could hear far better than he had ever been able to do before his accident. Each sound painted a picture in his mind until he could tell the difference between things in a way that he had never even noticed before. His ability to differentiate between so many aromas had become almost the same as actually seeing.

Almost.

Apart from game he had not killed anything and that troubled the man who had no other purpose in life. He was a hunter of men and that needed eyesight.

The legendary Iron Eyes had become a mere shadow of what he had once been and he knew it. He realized that once it became common knowledge that he was blind there would be many outlaws and even rival bounty hunters who would seek him out.

It was only a matter of time.

Some would consider that Iron Eyes was now nothing more than an easy notch to carve into their gun-grips. A trophy to be taken. Those who would never have dared even look at the gruesome thin figure when he could see would now wrongly think that killing him would be easy.

Iron Eyes was wary of this place. The wind made the only sound apart from the burning debris. He knew that if any of those who had destroyed this place were still around a man on a large palomino horse would make an easy target. He kept one hand on the reins ready to throw his thin frame back on top of the high saddle.

He cursed his blindness, for it had made him feel lost.

Lost in a whirlpool of blackness.

Iron Eyes had been riding through a land he did not recognize even by its perfume. He knew that he was heading into Mexico somewhere along its unmarked border, but where?

Only the stallion knew where they actually were.

Iron Eyes realized that he was headed to a place where he might be able to die. He had grown weary of living and if someone got the better of him, he was willing to accept that. For living had become too hard.

A man had to be a man in his book.

Drifting aimlessly was not what he did. He had become the hunter who was virtually unable to hunt. It had been a long while since he felt that he was anything but a ghost of what he had once been.

Maybe being shot down by a spineless coward was all he deserved. Iron Eyes thought it might be a mercy. Like putting a bullet in the head of a spent horse. Yet there was still the glowing embers of the fire which had fuelled his entire life smouldering deep in his innards. It would never allow someone to kill him if he had even the glimmer of a chance of killing them first.

There might be outlaws out there wanting to claim his scalp but they would have to fight damn hard to get it. Killing Iron Eyes, even a blind Iron Eyes, would not be as easy as it seemed.

Even ambushed the bounty hunter would go down shooting.

As the thin frail figure rested a hand upon the lowered neck of his drinking horse he wondered how long he would have to endure this long ride. How long would it be before one of the cowards got brave?

Iron Eyes moved to the nearer of his saddle-bags and skilfully found one of the whiskey bottles it contained. He shook the bottle next to his ear. It was a quarter full. His sharp teeth pulled its cork, then spat it away.

The glass neck of the bottle felt good against his scarred lips. He drank until every drople of the amber liquor had burned its way down into his guts before he tossed the bottle away.

The smashing glass made the horse beside him jump slightly but it continued drinking its fill from the trough.

Iron Eyes allowed the fumes of the whiskey to fill his head and drown his weariness. He wondered what had happened to this place filled with the smell of death. Who had died? How many bodies lay under the burning lumber which had once been a house?

He did not care who had done this awful thing. He knew there was no point in him getting riled up because he could do nothing about it. The killers had gone. Hours earlier. He could not capture them even if they were worth a fortune in bounty.

There had been a time when he could read the ground as well as any Apache tracker, but not now. The ground around him would have pointed the way he had to follow. He knew that it still did but he could not see it.

This burning and killing was still fresh though, his alert mind told him. Fresh enough to fill his flared nostrils with the stench only meat made when it was roasted. The stallion raised its head and gave out a satisfied snort.

'Reckon there ain't nothing we can do around here, horse,' Iron Eyes said before raising his pitifully thin left leg and poking his boot into the stirrup. 'There was a time when. . . .'

His words faded. He sat down on the saddle, pulled the reins up to him and went to wrap them around the saddle horn when something fifty feet from the trough caused his mount to turn its head.

'You heard it as well, huh?' Iron Eyes mumbled before hauling the powerful creature beneath him full circle. He listened as again he detected a sound he recognized. Someone was moving fast across the dried ground. Then there was another noise which the bounty hunter knew only too well.

It was the handguard of a repeating rifle being pushed down and then speedily raised back up. He heard a spent brass casing being ejected from the magazine of the primed weapon.

'Damn it,' Iron Eyes cursed as his bony hands tried to turn the palomino away from where he knew a rifle was being readied.

It was too late. He felt the heat of hot lead as it passed close to his hideous face. Then the sound of a Winchester blasting filled his ears and echoed all around the area. Another bullet followed in less than a heartbeat. It sent the stallion rearing up.

Iron Eyes attempted to hold on to the reins as the startled animal bucked. Another bullet ripped through the dry air and passed through the tails of his long trail coat as the bounty hunter felt himself losing contact with the high saddle.

The emaciated figure seemed to hover for a moment, then fall back down to where he had been standing seconds earlier. He crashed through a weathered hitching pole next to the trough and rolled forward. He could feel the hoofs of his horse pounding down into the ground beside him. Desperately Iron Eyes tried to reach the reins he knew must be close to those deadly hoofs, but he found nothing but dust. Another shot rang out and the horse bolted away from its master. Iron Eyes was winded but still capable of realizing that he was in trouble.

Big trouble.

His left hand dragged one of the Navy Colts from

his waist band and cocked its hammer. The light-weight weapon was ready for action.

So was Iron Eyes.

FOUR

The deafening tapers of white hot lead streaked and echoed across the ranch house clearing as they sought out the flesh and life of the bounty hunter. Fountains of water plumed upwards as the trough took the full force of the ferocious salvo. Chunks of razor-sharp splinters flew in all directions as the rifle bullets tore through the only object left unscathed by the earlier outrage. The cold water soaked the ground within a ten-foot circle of the place where Iron Eyes lay clutching his cocked weapon. In all his days he had never felt so totally helpless and alone.

Even his prized stallion had done the only sensible thing and fled. Iron Eyes hoped that none of his unknown adversaries bullets had hit the huge animal before it had managed to thunder away to safety.

Bullets.

Bullets which kept on coming in search of the man who was lying on his belly like a whipped hound.

36

Iron Eyes sucked air into his pitifully thin body and wondered if this was the end of his long sordid game. A game he had played for as long as he could recall. A game which had seen him dispatch so many wanted outlaws for the reward on their heads. Was this how it was going to end? Lying on his guts clutching one of his guns in his outstretched arm? A sad end to a sad existence was probably all he could expect. What else was there for a creature shunned by both red and white men alike?

He had been lucky to have lasted this long, he told himself.

Lucky still to be alive.

The redskins had always said he was a ghost. Not a real living man like them. A pathetic spectre who only killed because he was jealous of real living critters.

The bullets were getting closer. Dust was being kicked all over his prostrate form. If the bullets got any closer he knew he might end up permanently dead.

Why could he not see?

He could stare open-eyed at the blazing sun and not even make out a glimmer of light. Nothing.

That old doctor had promised him that his sight would return but his words had not become a reality. They had been lies. They had been nothing more than candy for a troublesome child. Words designed to calm a critter down to stop him destroying everything within reach as the fearful truth of his plight sunk in to his terrified mind. Nothing but candy.

There was a lull in the shooting.

The bounty hunter knew it meant the rifleman was reloading his weapon. With a reloaded weapon and a target lying out under the hot sun, it was time to move in for the kill. That is what hunters do. What he would do. You get your prey pinned down and defenceless and then come in to end it.

He raised his free hand and felt what was left of the cement skullcap. It was cracked and no longer fit for purpose but it was stuck good and hard to the long black hair that had continued to grow beneath its once protective cast.

Then his ears caught the sound of the safety guard of the Winchester being cranked into position. The rifle was loaded again. Time was running thin.

Iron Eyes squinted and desperately tried to force his eyes to see who it was out there. Yet he saw only blackness.

Sickening blackness.

'Who are you?' Iron Eyes yelled out loudly, trying to discover who his attacker was. 'What you damn well shooting at me for? I ain't worth wasting lead on. You hear me?'

There was no reply.

Again his keen hearing detected feet running across the ground to his right. He switched the Navy Colt to his other hand and tried to follow the movement with the long barrel of his primed weapon.

A thousand thoughts washed through his mind.

Twice as many questions.

Was this one of the vermin who had done this awful thing trying to add to the notches on his gun-grip?

That made no sense.

Why would any of the rustling killers remain here? They would have gone with the rest of their pack. Gone with the spoils of their mission. Only a locobean would remain here, to wait to kill anyone who might pass through this burned-out relic of a ranch.

His long gun-barrel still followed the feet he could hear racing from one place to another on the dried ground. His finger stroked the trigger but refused to pull back and fire until he knew who he was firing at.

It could not be any of the rustlers, he thought.

It had to be someone else.

Someone who was part of this ranch.

But that did not make any sense either.

Whoever had ridden into this once peaceful place had probably killed everyone before rustling off the steers. Why would they leave one person alive?

The question tormented him.

Another shot rang out.

Iron Eyes arched in pain as the bullet tore across the back of his coat. It cut through the frail fabric and ripped a trail across his shirt before burying itself into the ground beside him. Iron Eyes felt blood trickle down his bony back. He had been grazed. The rifleman had his range. Next time the bounty hunter knew that he might not be so lucky.

Iron Eyes used the toe of his right boot to swing his full length around. He trailed the footsteps with his keen hearing and kept the barrel of his weapon crudely aimed to where he thought his attacker might be.

'I oughta shoot you,' he mumbled. Then he considered. 'But what if'n you happen to be a snotnosed kid?'

That was it.

A snotnosed kid.

He listened hard. The footsteps were light. Like a young kid or maybe a female. No grown man with flesh on his bones sounded as light as that, he considered. Not unless his name was Iron Eyes.

Normal folks had muscle. Their footsteps sound heavy. Rustlers who came on horseback wore spurs. Again he heard no spurs. He was pinned down by a young buck.

What should he do? Iron Eyes did not want to kill any child if he could help it. Not even if the child was getting damn close to killing him. He tried to think as sweat traced down his scarred features.

'My name's Iron Eyes,' he shouted out. 'I don't mean you no harm.'

The runner paused. Iron Eyes swung around

40

again, keeping his gun aimed to where he could tell the shooter rested.

He had to be right. It was the only thing which made sense.

The person who had opened up on him must belong to all the dead folks he could smell burning in the ashes of the ranch house. A kid. A kid who had not actually seen who had killed his kinfolk but figured it had to be the macabre figure of Iron Eyes.

Why had he not been killed with the others?

Iron Eyes crawled back to where he could hear the water pouring out from the bullet holes in the trough. The water was cool and welcoming as his tall skinny figure pushed himself against the only cover the yard had to offer.

Then it dawned on him. The kid must have been off somewhere else when this outrage had occurred.

'Hunting,' Iron Eyes whispered. 'He was off hunting with his rifle when this happened.'

Suddenly the blind figure knew he was right.

Knew he had solved the puzzle.

The deadly problem still existed though. Whoever it was shooting at him had not had time to think. Not had time coldly to evaluate the situation as he had done. The shooter's mind was fuelled by grief. The bounty hunter knew only too well that sometimes grief could make a critter as blind as he was.

Blind to everything but revenge.

It was a sin he himself had fallen in to many times.

Even a child could kill when his heart had been broken, Iron Eyes resolved. There were many types of blindness. His present disability was only just one of them.

'Listen up. You don't want to kill me,' the bounty hunter called out.

Once more there was no response. No reply.

Iron Eyes pressed his bleeding back against the trough. The water washed over his wound. There was another thing he had to worry about, he told himself. Even if it was just a kid shooting at him, that kid had a repeating rifle whilst he only had a six-shooter.

The shooter had sight.

He was blind.

One mighty big disadvantage.

'I'm in a heap of real bad trouble here.' Iron Eyes sighed wistfully to himself.

Then two more shots rang out in quick succession, but Iron Eyes only heard the first. That one hit the edge of the trough and sent splinters exploding into the hot air. The second knocked Iron Eyes completely senseless as it brutally glanced across the top of his cement skullcap, leaving it cracked in two. Two segments that refused to drop from the head of matted hair of which it had become part.

His bony fingers released their grip on the six-shooter. The Navy Colt dropped limply from his hand. Iron Eyes rocked on his knees as a line of blood ran down his hideous face. He then slumped forward.

He fell face first into the wet sand.

Iron Eyes did not hear the approaching footsteps, nor the Winchester being cocked again.

FIVE

Mason Burr had risen earlier than most in the remote border town because he had achieved his goal. Finished his crimson-stained business with cold-hearted precision. Destroyed more innocents and pocketed their hard-earned life savings. It was time to move on to his next goal. The well-dressed man had washed the gore from his hands as well as his memory. Now in his finest travelling clothes he headed on down Main Street as though nothing had happened the previous evening. The scent of his freshly pomaded hair drifted on the morning breeze and found the noses of the town's womenfolk. They gushed as he smiled and touched the brim of his brushed hat. None of them realized that the appearance of respectability was like the cover of a book. It seldom denoted what lay inside the pages of the tome.

There had been an eerie quiet around Rio Bravos,

44

which only Burr sensed. He was calm as always, as though defying the heat of the morning sunshine which burned down upon the remote town. Men like Burr refused to sweat like lesser mortals.

After lighting a stout cigar and gripping it between his teeth Burr had left his hotel and methodically made his way along the boardwalk towards the stage-coach depot. He had already calculated to the exact number of strides the short journey would entail.

He would have preferred a train to aid his flight from yet another town and the grisly evidence he had left three streets behind his highly polished footwear. The two bodies were curled up in the parlour of the banker's house, where he had slain them less than eight hours earlier. Horace Grimes and his doting spouse had paid the ultimate price for their generosity towards and curiosity about the elegant stranger. Like so many of Grimes's breed the lure of easy money had been too much. He had also trusted his eyes rather than his brain. Surely, gentlemen dressed like Burr and with impeccable manners could not possibly be anything other than what they appeared to be.

It was a fatal mistake so many others had made.

Burr had smiled his way into their confidence. Smiled with a fistful of forged mortgages which he had claimed he was going to have to sell due to a temporary cashflow problem. As always it had worked a treat. It had opened all doors into the

THE SHADOW OF IRON EYES

banker's greedy soul and had allowed the deadly confidence trickster to get close to his prey.

There was no sign of guilt in the face of the man
who had used his unchallenged ability to trick and
then kill the couple in their quaint whitewashed
home. To Burr they had got what they deserved
because he had always managed to justify his lethal
deeds to himself.

The old saying that you cannot con an honest man
was the only rule he lived by. To Burr it was the truth.
The only truth. The banker had thought he was
going to make a killing at the cost of the handsome
visitor to his home; to take advantage of a man who
claimed to be in desperate need of money.

Burr knew that all bankers had more than their
share of avarice flowing through their veins. Grimes
had been made to pay dearly for that Biblical sin.

Horace Grimes had almost drooled when he had
greeted his guest, knowing that he was on the verge
of making a killing. Unfortunately for the banker it
had been Mason Burr who had made the killing,
both financially and literally. As always there had
been no witnesses to the gruesome action. No proof
that the man in the well-tailored suit had even been
there at all.

The heavy canvas valise was gripped firmly in his
strong left hand as Burr stepped down and crossed
the dusty street towards the six-horse team being
backed into the traces of the waiting stagecoach.

Apart from the driver there would be no one else on this journey away from yet another ghastly killing. Burr liked that as he stepped up and watched the two sweat-soaked liverymen rubbing their massive hands down their shirts before heading back to where the stable stood high behind the depot.

Smoke curled from his lips.

Burr knew that he would have hours yet before anyone even missed Grimes. All bankers were the same. They let their underlings open up the bank and do their work whilst they lingered in their homes and sipped on another cup of coffee. No one would realize until the stagecoach was far beyond the long arms of retribution that anything was wrong at all. Not until it was too late. It would probably be another hour before they could raise the sheriff from his cot and take him to the banker's house. Another hour before the lawman could justify in his own mind the actions he would require to break into the house. A house which seemed perfectly normal.

Burr smiled to himself. It was a sickly smile such as only killers have ever truly mastered. He ambled along the boardwalk and leaned on the doorframe of the depot. His eyes looked in at the depot manager, who was standing next to the dishevelled driver.

'Howdy.' The manager smiled. 'If'n you happen to be looking for a stage then you surely come to the right place.'

Burr tilted his head. 'You don't happen to go to El

47

Remo, do you?'

Both men looked at Burr. The depot manager shook his head.

'Nope. That's south of the border, friend. The closest we goes to El Remo is Cooperville. That's a good ten or so miles shy. You'll have to hire a buggy or horse to get to El Remo.'

'Then how much is it for a one way ticket to Cooperville?' Burr asked, tapping grey ash from his cigar.

The driver brushed past Burr and made his way out to check the team of fresh horses. The man with the black visor on his brow thought for a moment. 'That'll be exactly fifteen dollars, friend.'

Burr's smile grew wider.

'Cheap at half the price.' Burr said as his fingers sought and found a golden half-eagle in his vest pocket. 'When does the stage head on out?'

The depot man looked at the wall clock and then back at the man before him. 'Five minutes, or when Rufas gets his sorry arse up on that seat.'

Burr handed the coin over and looked at the driver as the stocky broad-shouldered man started the long climb up to his lofty perch. 'No stagecoach guard?'

'Ain't no call,' the depot man said. He bit the gold coin, dropped it into his cash drawer and scooped out his passenger's change and a ticket. 'Only use a guard when there's a strongbox on board. Hell, you're the only valuable thing on the whole coach this morning, mister.'

'Does the coach stop along the way?' Burr enquired.

'Yep,' the man replied before licking the lead of his pencil. 'There's a couple of way stations between here and Cooperville. You'll have time to get a few snorts and some mighty fine vittles.'

Burr accepted the handful of coins and smiled through his cigar smoke. 'Perfect.'

'Going to El Remo on business, friend?' the depot man asked as he started scratching on his ledger.

Mason Burr pocketed the loose change, sighed, then turned his head. His merciless eyes watched the driver like an eagle studying unsuspecting prey. 'Indeed.'

SIX

A long black shadow crept slowly across the sun-baked ground towards the bullet-ridden water trough and the grim vision lying before it. Blood encircled the prostrated form. Blood which seeped from the shattered cement skull cap upon the mane of matted hair belonging to the unconscious bounty hunter. The wet ground had willingly accepted the cruelly scarred face which had fallen upon it only moments earlier. Like a mask of death it had moulded its damp, choking sand around every brutally scarred feature of his face. The Winchester bullet had hit him hard as it smashed across the cement surface of the crude head protection. Unknown to the suffocating Iron Eyes the clumsy device designed to hold his shattered skull together until it healed had again saved his life.

Yet the sheer power of the impact had caused every part of his brain to temporarily cease functioning.

50

Everything had stopped in an unholy white flash. There were no thoughts. No fear or anger coursing through his mind. It had all stopped. Only a dead man might have had less on his mind than Iron Eyes had at that very instant. It was as though he had been head-butted by a raging bull. The fragile line between life and death was now blurred into a terrifying whirlpool of flashing lights. Sticks of dynamite exploded inside his skull as if something was trying to bring him back from the abyss he was staring into with blind eyes.

No bloodied prize fighter who had caught a clenched fist of hardened knuckles on his chin could have fallen into such a place, a place where Iron Eyes was drowning in a quagmire of wet choking sand. The bounty hunter's nostrils and mouth were sucking in sand as his body instinctively fought to save itself.

His entire body began to shake in uncontrollable spasms as it battled to find air amid the fine granules of sand. To the curious eyes of the onlooker who had done this to the bounty hunter it seemed as though invisible strings were tugging at the otherwise lifeless body.

Even unconscious Iron Eyes was fighting. Fighting to survive long enough to wake up from this devilish nightmare. Fighting for his very life. Yet the more his long limbs feverishly shook the more sand was sucked into his feeble face. Blood trailed from the cracked cement and ran along the strands of his limp black hair and out on to the damp ground.

Then the rifle-toting shadow loomed over his helpless body and aimed the barrel straight at the back of his head.

For a few moments the figure just watched. Watched in total confusion.

The shaking outstretched body seemed neither dead nor alive to the slim figure who kept the smoking rifle barrel trained on its target. Were these the death throes of a man? Like you see when you chop the head off a chicken and it runs around for long minutes, realizing that it's dead?

Or was this something else?

Something the eyes of the person holding the Winchester had never witnessed before. Was the creature lying face down in its own blood dead or was it just stunned?

Some critters never seem to know when to die. Was this man one of those? The kind that are just too stupid to know they are dead? Too stubborn to figure out they ought to quit and carry on their journey either to heaven or hell. Was that it?

The thumb pulled back on the rifle hammer again.

Maybe it needed another bullet to end its misery. Few folks, even hunters, have the stomach to watch any critter suffer.

The onlooker could not tell.

'Get up,' the voice demanded. A well-placed shoe-less foot struck hard into the ribs of Iron Eyes. There appeared to be no response.

Iron Eyes continued to twitch and shake as the sound of his lungs sucking in sand grew louder and more desperate.

'You hear me? Get the hell up before I puts a bullet through ya neck.'

There was no reaction to the words because Iron Eyes had not heard any of them. They could not compete with the massive explosions that were going off inside his head. The bounty hunter had other far more urgent things to trouble himself about.

He was drowning in an inch of wet sand.

The hand of the shadow reached down until its fingers caught hold of the long black hair protruding from the cement cast. It twisted and turned its length until it was wrapped around its slim wrist. It violently tugged the head up out of the choking sand and then eased the bounty hunter on to his side.

At first there was no sign of life as the hands and feet slowly stopped shaking.

Then a massive cough came from Iron Eyes and shook his entire length. Lumps of wet sand were propelled from his wide open mouth across the yard.

He then rolled over on to his back.

'Holy smoke.' The man holding the long-barrelled rifle panted in horror at the sight. 'Ain't you just the ugliest critter?'

Unknown to the startled onlooker the bounty hunter heard each of the choice words. Iron Eyes was awake. Awake to listen to the war drums which pounded out a beat inside his fractured head as one by one his senses rekindled.

'I oughta shoot ya.' The words filled the aching head of the man lying outstretched on the sand. 'By the looks of ya it would be merciful.'

With the speed of a sidewinder, Iron Eyes suddenly clawed out with his talon-like fingers. His bony digits found the nearer of the speaker's legs and grabbed the ankle. With every ounce of his strength he jerked his arm back towards his bleeding body. He heard the startled yelp, then felt the impact of the lean figure as it landed next to him. The long barrel of the Winchester hit him full in his sand-covered face, but Iron Eyes did not feel any pain. He grabbed at the weapon and hurled it away.

'Kill me?' Iron Eyes spat sand with each word. 'I reckon you don't know the difference between a wounded critter and a dead'un when you see one, boy.'

Fists flew back and forth in both directions as the pair scrambled on the damp ground like fighting dogs. Both heads were jolted back as glancing blows found their targets. Nails clawed at the bounty hunter's face but Iron Eyes did not feel anything. He punched out, felt the impact on his bony knuckles. He knew that he had stunned his foe. He might have been blind but he was still a lethal killer. A hunter honed like a straight razor. He knew that he could kill this youngster at any time he wished but the scent of death still lingered inside his guts. Another pointless slaying would be one too many. Besides, he only killed wanted men for the reward money on their heads. There was no profit in killing anyone else.

He wrestled the still-fighting figure and forced the shoulders down. He then swung his thin legs over and dropped on top of his victim. He had the varmint pinned down. Pinned down but the fists kept pounding into his chest and face at an alarming rate.

'Quit hitting me,' Iron Eyes ordered in vain.

Like the stings of a whole swarm of hornets even more punches showered into the battered bounty hunter. There was only one way to stop this, Iron Eyes thought.

With the speed of a lightning bolt Iron Eyes's right hand reached back and found his deadly Bowie knife in the neck of his mule-ear boot. He dragged it free and swiftly brought it up to the face of the firecracker he was sitting astride.

This required both hands. One to act as his eyes and the other to manoeuvre and press the blade under the chin against the soft young flesh.

'Quit fighting or I'll cut ya damn head clean off, boy.'

'Stop!' the voice screamed out as Iron Eyes's knife-blade rested against the throat. 'Don't cut my head off.'

For a moment both combatants rested, trying to get their second wind and thinking of what to do next. The bounty hunter felt a sudden pain rip through his brain. It was like a bullet cutting its way through flesh. He tried to shake it away but it kept stabbing into his pounding head. Then the drumming seemed to fade for a while.

'You OK, mister?' There was a hint of concern in the voice. There was also something else about the voice that he had not noticed before.

Something strange. Something which stunned Iron Eyes.

'Don't kill me.' The voice was begging now,

'You wanted dead or alive?' Iron Eyes asked.

'Nope.'

'You an Apache wanting to kill old Iron Eyes?'

'I don't reckon.'

'Then I ain't gonna kill ya.'

'Then why ya still sitting on me, Iron Eyes?' The voice was agitated.

'To stop ya killing me, young 'un.' Iron Eyes muttered and then felt a burning in his eyes. They still refused to work but they were aching. 'You come a lot closer to killing me than most folks ever done. I gotta be sure that ya ain't gonna try to finish the job.'

'You one of the critters who killed my family?' It was not the question which stunned the bounty hunter, it was the voice itself.

The voice of a female.

56

Iron Eyes rested on top of the outstretched body. His gritted teeth parted as the truth dawned on him. That was what was wrong with the voice. It was not a young boy who had almost blown his head off his shoulders but a female of unguessable years.

'You a girl?' he stammered unable to accept what his ears were telling him. This was a female. There was something in the determined voice. A pitch that was a tad higher than even of the littlest of boys he had ever heard.

'Sure I'm a girl.' The angry words came with a good amount of spittle. Spittle which clung to the face of the man who was still keeping the blade of his trusty knife pressing into her throat just in case she still managed to get the better of him. 'But that don't amount to nothing in these parts. I can still best most menfolk. Beat them into a bloody pulp.'

Iron Eyes could still feel blood tracing from his back and his head. There was no way he was going to argue with this critter. He continued to sit on his victim as his mind raced in a vain attempt to figure out what he should do now. Was she finished? He doubted it. Would she shoot him if she had a chance? He reckoned it was a fair bet. Any normal man might have released her but not Iron Eyes. Being unable to see made him even more wary. She had already proved that she was deadly, given half a chance. Only a locobean would trust her not to try and finish off the job she had started on the infamous bounty hunter.

57

He still did not want to release his grip until he was certain that she was beaten.

'You sure that you ain't a boy?' he whispered.

'Do I look like a boy?' More spittle hit his blank features.

'Why'd ya shoot at me?' he growled. His free hand roamed over her shirt until the evidence of her gender became more apparent to his sensitive fingertips. 'OK. Ya feels like a gal. But how come ya dressed like a man? You sure that you're a girl and not some kind of freak?'

'Freak?' Her voice was raised far louder than the man with the war drums inside his skull had expected. He rocked on his knees. 'Who ya calling a freak?'

'You.' His hands kept investigating her chest. It was obvious that she wore no undergarments beneath her well-worn shirt. The wounded Iron Eyes was not sure whether he actually liked the experience or not. He had never been so close to a female before.

She started to pound on his pitifully thin chest and then tried to claw at his eyes. 'I ain't dressed like no man. These is my hunting clothes. Are ya blind?'

'Kinda.' There was a sorrowful sound to his voice.

'What?' She stared up at the creature who was astride her slim form as though she were a filly and he were a rider. 'Ya mean ya can't see nothing?'

'Not a damn thing.' His hands returned to her

58

pert breasts hidden beneath the worn shirt.

She began to wriggle. 'Blind or not, I'd thank you to kindly stop feeling me like that.'

'I gotta feel ya,' Iron Eyes snarled. 'Gotta check you're telling the truth.'

'I'm starting to get a little troubled by the curiosity in them damn fingers of yours, Iron Eyes.' Her voice went up a little as she began actually to enjoy the way his innocent hands were manipulating her bosoms in turn, as though they had never encountered any such before. 'It ain't righteous for a man to do that to a gal's chest. Not with his cotton-picking hands, anyways. Are you damn sure that you're blind?'

The bounty hunter realized what he was doing. He lifted his hand away and rubbed his blood covered face.

'I can't see nothing,' he admitted. 'Nothing at all.'

There was a long pause as she stared at his hideous face and for the first time noticed how his bullet-coloured eyes stared off into the distance as he spoke.

'Ya mean that you're blind as well as ugly?'

'Reckon so.'

'Lady Luck sure dealt you a mighty poor hand there, mister.'

He nodded. 'Yep.'

'How come ya didn't shoot back at me, Iron Eyes?' she asked quietly. 'I thought ya would open up with them hoglegs of yours but you just let me shoot

59

chunks off ya worthless hide.'

'I never waste bullets on folks who ain't outlaws.' Iron Eyes slid the Bowie knife back down into the neck of his boot. 'I should have killed ya for what you done to me, though.'

She raised both eyebrows. 'I thought ya was one of the bastards that done for my kinfolk and then set fire to the house, mister.'

There was a smouldering inside the bounty hunter to equal that which was still consuming what was left of the house timbers. He had nothing but contempt for anyone who killed innocents.

'Vermin. Them rustlers were nothing but vermin.' Iron Eyes carefully stood up and rubbed the sand from his hideous features. His long thin legs were planted on either side of her. He listened to her as she crawled out from between his boots and scrambled to her feet. 'I'm sorry I didn't get here a whole lot sooner, girl. Even blind I might have bin able to kill a few of the varmints.'

For a few seconds she just brushed her pants down and watched the strange emaciated figure who seemed totally lost in a world he was unable to figure out any longer.

'How come you can't see?' she asked.

'Had my skull caved in.' A long thin digit gestured towards his head. 'The old sawbones who fixed me up said that my eyes might start working again. Reckon he was just sweet-talking me.'

'My name's Sally.' She told him bashfully. 'I'm of age.'

'What?' Iron Eyes did not understand.

A wry smile illuminated her face. 'I'm a grown woman.'

'Ya chest is sure full grown,' Iron Eyes muttered.

Her expression altered. She brought her leg back angrily and then swung it at full force towards his groin. Her foot caught Iron Eyes between his legs. He had not seen it coming but he sure felt it when it arrived. He coughed and then buckled until his head was almost level with his knees. He felt sick as he staggered a few steps toward her.

'W-what ya do that for?' he gasped, holding his manhood with both hands.

'That's for feeling my chest when we hadn't bin properly introduced, Iron Eyes,' she replied. She turned on her heel and began to march away from him.

'I ain't planning to do it again,' he said, quailing.

Sally paused suddenly. 'There ain't no need for ya to go all mulish, Iron Eyes. I didn't say ya couldn't do it again if'n ya'd a mind to romancing.'

'Ain't much of a chest anyways.' He spat the words.

'Ya must be a darn lucky critter by all accounts.' She resumed marching away from him. 'Yep. Darn lucky.'

Iron Eyes nursed his crotch in bewilderment at her utterance. 'How do ya figure that?'

61

As she started to fill the yard with youthful laughter she added. 'Ya lucky I ain't got no shoes on. Yep, you sure would be whistling Dixie in a whole different key if'n I had me my shoes on. They got pointed toes.'

A hurting Iron Eyes managed to straighten up. He was about to respond when he noticed a faint flickering of light penetrating the darkness in his left eye. His heart began to race. He turned and then tilted his head back. Iron Eyes winced when the sun hit his face. A crooked smile etched his face.

'Thank ya kindly, Sal,' he drawled.

SEVEN

The afternoon sun was ferocious. Mercilessly, it baked everything along the barren trail between Rio Bravos and Cooperville to a cinder. Only cactus and Joshua trees managed to survive its daily unyielding onslaught. It was said that the Devil himself had designed this land, and those who travelled its length would have agreed. It was an unholy place set only a handful of miles away from verdant, more hospitable terrain. What water there was came from deep wells dug out by desperate men generations earlier. That was the main reason why there were only two way stations along the trail through the parched landscape. A lot of men had died digging dry holes before a couple of them had got lucky and discovered the precious liquid they sought.

The dust-caked stagecoach had just left the way station at Adobe Flats with a fresh team of six sturdy horses pulling the virtually empty conveyance behind their black tails. It was heading on through yet more parched terrain along the unmarked border to Mexico. Its intended destination was Cooperville. It would never reach its goal.

Mason Burr had other plans for the well-sprung coach in which he rode as its driver guided the eager team on towards the place where the sand was renowned for being the colour of fresh blood. High scarlet mesas loomed like silent giants overlooking the well-used trail that cut between their towering walls. The shimmering heat along the trail could reach unimaginable temperatures and was capable of roasting the flesh off the bones of anything dead or alive. This was a place where only serpents had a chance of survival, and yet even they remained hidden during the daylight hours.

But men had left their mark here. As clouds of dust were kicked up by the stagecoach's wheels and hung in the dry air the solitary passenger studied the line of telegraph poles which lined the route. Poles, now bleached white by the incessant sun, had been erected as if they alone might bring civilization to this unforgiving land. Their glistening wires never moved as they stretched from one pole to another: wires which could send invisible messages from one town to the next and far beyond. These messages had caught out many fleeing killers.

Mason Burr knew that hours earlier, when they had departed from Rio Bravos, his crime was still undetected. The bodies of Horace Grimes and his obedient spouse still lay undiscovered in the parlour of their house. The wall safe in that parlour now lay empty.

No rider could ever have managed to catch up with the stagecoach as it started on its final leg of the long journey between towns, but a simple message sent out from Rio Bravos along those wires would take only heartbeats to reach Cooperville and its lawmen.

From the carriage window Burr glared at those poles and their wires with a hatred he usually reserved for his victims. He knew that they could be his downfall if he actually went to the town for which he had purchased his ticket. He knew that his appearance of respectability might be in his favour, but the money and other valuable items he had taken from Grimes's home were still in his bag. Their presence could hang him.

It was a risk Burr was unwilling to take.

Besides, he had a previously arranged appointment in El Remo with another potential victim. South of the border there was no law to speak of. Not in El Remo, anyway.

The well-dressed man had returned to the well-sprung comfort inside the fast-moving vehicle before the coach had set out from Adobe Flats. Yet even dressed in his finery, Burr had never had any intention of remaining inside the coach.

Now it was time for him to act.

Despite his gentlemanly appearance Mason Burr was still a very agile man who had well-disguised physical prowess, which he was about to exercise. He placed his hat down next to his canvas valise and started to remove his coat and silk-lined vest, making sure that his hidden holster with its well-used firearm remained under his armpit. The string tie was removed from his starched collar and carefully placed inside the pocket of his vest. Burr then moved from one side of the coach to the other and glanced down at the shadow on the ground. The driver's outline told him exactly where his next victim was.

Burr rolled up his sleeves and opened his bag. The dagger was small but lethally effective. Dried blood along its otherwise pristine blade gave evidence of what it had only recently been used for. He pushed it down into his pants belt, then placed a hand on the door handle.

They were getting closer to the spot where Burr knew it was a mere three miles to El Remo. All he had to do was take control of the stagecoach and head there.

That and kill the driver.

For a man with as much blood filling his shadowy past another murder was nothing to fret about. It was a means to an end. The simplest of solutions. Nothing to cause him to lose even a second's sleep when he was able to rest his head later that night.

Burr pushed the door open and allowed it to rest against the body of the fast-moving coach. Dust rose up as the well-built man reached upwards for the metal rail which ran round the roof of the stage. There was no fear in the heartless soul of the deadly killer, only total belief in his ability.

Burr stretched up and curled his fingers around the metal rail. He gripped it firmly, then hoisted himself out through the window. His foot rested in the window's frame. It had been a while since Burr had last attempted anything quite so energetic but he had lost none of his agility.

Like a mountain cat he had scaled the side of the stagecoach over the smaller front wheel within seconds. The dust blowing into his mouth and eyes did not cause him a moment's pause.

There was a deed to be done.

A deathly job the notion of which few would have had the stomach even to entertain. He required control of the stagecoach and knew in his hardened soul that the driver would not willingly allow him to achieve his goal.

With his hefty right boot resting upon the brake pole, Rufas Day brought the heavy reins down across the backs of the thundering team and urged them on to even greater pace. They were fresh and eager to oblige. Then out of the corner of his eye Rufas caught sight of his passenger appearing from over the side of the rocking stagecoach. He watched in total confusion as Burr sat down beside him.

'W-what ya doing, man?' the driver shouted out as dust filled his gaping mouth.

Silently Mason Burr slid his rump closer to Rufas Day.

'Ya ain't meant to be up here, fella,' the driver added.

The blade of the knife glinted in the burning rays of the sun above them. Rufas Day screwed up his dust-filled eyes and looked down at it. He was about to speak when Burr thrust his arm out and buried the weapon deep into the driver's chest. A groan whispered from the mouth of Rufas Day as his life ended.

Crimson gore flowed over Burr's hand. It meant nothing to the man who valued nothing but his own life. He tugged the knife back out of the driver's chest and took the reins from the lifeless hands. It was easy to push the dead body off its high seat. He did not see or hear it hit the ground but continued to whip the reins down across the backs of the thundering six-horse team.

He dragged the reins hand to his left.

He was now heading for El Remo.

EIGHT

El Remo was what it had always been: a cesspit which no respectable person would ever visit willingly. Most of its population lived off the spoils of the bandits and outlaws who used it as a safe haven. El Remo was a place where the only law was gun law. Three-quarters of the people who lived within its sprawling boundaries were pure-blood Mexican. A handful were Indians who had been expelled from their various tribes, and the remainder were Stetson-wearing white men. This was a town just south of the Texas border and every one of its occupants exploited that fact to the fullest degree. So close, and yet it was a million miles from the justice its northern neighbour was famed for. After numerous revolutions the Mexican authorities had almost melted into the hot sand. El Remo was trouble and whoever was in charge of the government wanted nothing to do with it and those who lived in it.

The town itself was perched on a high cliff rising above boulders the size of houses. The embankments led down to an estuary said to feed into the Rio Grande but no one knew for sure. A huge cave opened up halfway down the side of the treacherous slope; it was reputed to be the entrance to a maze of tunnels. The deadly rocky terrain looked as though it had been created by some long-extinct burrowing monster.

Few ventured anywhere near the cave even though it was rumoured that its walls were dripping with golden nuggets ripe for picking. The chance of becoming rich overnight had never appealed to any of those who filled the whorehouses and saloons of El Remo, though. They liked their pickings to come easy rather than actually risking breaking out in a sweat.

A stench of limeless outhouses filled the dry sun-baked air that hung over the large danger-ridden settlement. It repelled most, yet lured others. This was a town which was ruled by a mere handful of people more lethal than most in the neighbouring West.

Fights and gun wars erupted almost daily as one gang was set against a rival by their paymasters. Blood stained the sandy streets all through El Remo. It seemed pointless even trying to clean up the brutal evidence of one fight as there was always another only a matter of hours away from starting.

The town itself looked as if it ought to be in Texas, not Mexico. Most of its buildings were wooden and brick and what adobe structures it still boasted remained on its very outskirts. A myriad flies buzzed their way through the unkempt thoroughfares. A similar number of rats hid beneath squalid buildings.

The men and women who lived here knew that this was a place where their kind fitted in just fine. The flies and the rodents were a lot easier to handle than the lawmen who filled most of the towns to the north. These reprobates were a breed apart and, whatever their colour or creed, they knew that they never had to fear who might come calling with a Wanted poster in their greedy hand.

Death came swiftly in El Remo but it was a death they understood. A death upon which, if they were quick enough, they might turn the tables. Kill before being killed was the only sensible course any of them could take. They had reached the end of the road when they had drawn rein in El Remo. The only place left for their kind to go to from here was Hell itself.

In all the years El Remo had existed no honest soul had ever dared to come into its dangerous midst. Only those as bad as the two legged vermin who were already there were welcome. There was an unspoken rule in the town and that was one they all lived by.

Shoot low, they might be crawling.

The stagecoach had caused a lot of interest as it sped along the winding streets after passing the unmarked boundaries of El Remo. It was not usual to see a stagecoach anywhere south of the border, especially one with Overland Stagecoach Company painted on its livery. The solitary driver drew less interest amongst the thousands of onlookers. When you had seen one dust-caked man, you had seen them all.

There was logic in their seeming lack if interest. Whoever it was on the high driver's seat, he had to be cut from the same cloth as themselves.

No honest man ever came to El Remo.

They just imagined that one of their own had managed to steal the huge vehicle and its six-horse team and had then decided to bring it to town.

Mason Burr hauled back on the reins and pushed his right leg down against the brake pole as the rocking coach reached the busiest part of El Remo.

Dust kicked up off the wheels and the hoofs of the horses as the vehicle skidded the last twenty yards of its journey until it finally halted. The stagecoach was still rocking on its weary springs as Burr climbed down to the ground. He opened the nearest carriage door and withdrew his vest and coat before placing his hat upon his head and retrieving his canvas valise.

It might have said cantina on the bullet-hole-ridden façade but it was a saloon. Just as he was about to step up on to the boardwalk Burr tilted his head and gave the balcony a fleeting glance. Half a dozen females were hanging over its rail in various stages of undress. He could smell their powder and war paint. Burr smiled and touched his hat brim. This weathered building was also a whorehouse, he surmised.

'What you want here?' a man with two belts of bullets crossing his massive chest asked in a Mexican accent whilst gripping his holstered .44.

Burr paused and sucked in his belly. He studied the man beneath the black sombrero carefully.

'I'm here on business,' he announced loud enough for half the street to hear. 'Out of my way.'

The large man was not impressed. He held out a hand at chest level and stopped Burr from reaching the boardwalk. 'I ask you again, *señor*. What you want here?'

'I'm here to meet Mexican Pete,' Burr growled. 'Now out of my way or you will regret your interference.'

The man pushed his sombrero back off his dirt-stained face and screwed up his eyes. 'I no like Mexican Pete, *señor*. I think I no like you.'

'I imagine Pete does not like you either.' Burr started to button up his vest front and then faster than any of the gathered crowd would think possible, he drew the hidden gun from under his armpit. He cocked and fired it three times in quick succession, then stepped to the side like a matador. There was no heart capable of withstanding a trio of bullets tearing into it. A stunned expression filled the rugged features of the man beneath the sombrero. His massive form staggered as smoke came from the neatly grouped bullet holes in his chest followed by streams of blood. He then tumbled forward and crashed down into the street like a felled tree.

'Mexican Pete ain't in town,' a voice announced.

'No matter. I can wait.' Mason Burr looked around at the scores of faces watching him and blew down the barrel of the small weapon. 'Let that be a lesson to all of you. Mason Burr don't take prisoners.'

Every eye watched the confident trickster as he stepped over the body and mounted the steps until he reached the boardwalk and the swing doors which led to a place almost as aromatic as the street.

Burr entered.

There were no other obstacles.

Iron Eyes dragged the heavy Mexican saddle off the back of the palomino stallion and dropped it on to the sun-hardened ground at his feet next to his saddle-bags. He then looped his long reins around the saddle horn and secured them.

'That'll stop ya high-tailing it again, horse,' the bounty hunter told the tall animal. 'Damn coward. Leaving me to face all that lead alone. She nearly killed me.'

The horse snorted and dragged a hoof across the ground.

'You ain't thanked me for catching that nag of yours yet, Iron Eyes,' Sally commented from where she was kneeling beside a small campfire. 'He'd not have come back on his own, ya know.'

Iron Eyes shrugged. 'OK. OK. Thank ya kindly for catching my horse for me.'

'My pleasure.' She grinned.

'He'd not have run off if'n you hadn't been shooting at me though,' the lean figure added.

Sally turned the crude wooden spit which she had erected over the flames of the small fire before her. Their supper was nearly cooked. 'You ain't gonna ever quit complaining about me shooting at you, are ya?'

Iron Eyes exhaled loudly. 'Not while I'm still bleeding, gal.'

Smoke rose from the destroyed buildings in the yard as the flames finally died out. The bounty hunter knew that there was nothing left for them to feed upon. All the timber and flesh had been consumed. Blackened ashes hissed like a bag of rattlers as the tall, long-legged figure looked up to where his skin told him the sun was. A faint glimmer of light was still managing to find its way through his left eye and tell his brain that his days of blindness might soon be ending.

'You sure are a strange critter,' Sally remarked for the umpteenth time. 'You just keep looking at the sun and yet them eyes of yours can't see the damn thing.'

75

Iron Eyes did not speak. He had no intention of celebrating something which he knew from experience might be short-lived. His eyes had fooled him before. Made him believe they were healed and that he was about to regain his sight only then to suddenly return him to the black despair of blindness.

He lowered his head, then turned to face her. He could vaguely see the flames. His entire body turned as he sniffed the air. There was something familiar about the aroma coming from the little campfire. Something he recalled from his youth. He knew the scent of whatever it was she was roasting.

'Smells good,' Iron Eyes heard himself say.

'It'll taste better,' Sally assured him.

He gave a long sigh and tried to work out roughly how long there was until the sun would set. An hour? Maybe a tad more. Not that it mattered to a blind man. This was a strange country and he knew it well. It would burn the skin off a man's back during the day and then try to freeze him to death during the long nights. Recently, since he had lost his sight, Iron Eyes had started to travel on his lonely journey during the nights. It made little odds to a man who could not see whether it was day or night and if you rode through the night you could fend off the cold a little.

'It'll be dark soon,' he observed.

'You gonna marry me?' Her question seemed tinted with a girlish humour which the tall man could not comprehend. 'Are ya, Iron Eyes?'

His head turned until his face was aimed at her kneeling on the ground. 'What?'

'I'm of age,' she added. 'And besides, I might be with child and a man has to do the right thing.'

'With child?' He heard himself repeat her words. 'How?'

'Well, ya was having ya fun with me.' She was careful not to let him hear the giggles she suppressed. 'Sitting on me and riding me like I was a mustang to be broke. Yep. And you was feeling me all over and ya liked it. That's how babies is made, ain't it?'

'I don't reckon so.' Iron Eyes swallowed hard.

'Me an orphan and you a wild lustful creature.' She continued to add fuel to the fire, 'How could ya? Ain't ya ashamed?'

'What?' Iron Eyes carefully allowed the rest of his lean body to follow the boot toes. 'Are you serious, girl?'

'Sally,' she corrected loudly. 'I told ya my name's Sally. Not gal or girl. My name's Sally. Sally Cooke.'

His footsteps were measured as he closed the distance between them. 'You don't truly think that's how babies is made, do ya, Sally? Do ya?'

There was a long silence, then she began to giggle.

'Nope. I sure don't.' She burst out laughing. 'I ain't stupid. I seen how critters do it. We had us a bull once who—'

'Stop joshing with me,' Iron Eyes shouted at her. 'I'm still bleeding from them damn shots ya hit me with. My head got a whole war party beating drums inside it and you keep trying to rile me up. Ain't ya ashamed?'

'Nope.'

'I thought folks who just lost kin was meant to be sad,' he observed. 'Not joshing and the like.'

'I'm crying, Iron Eyes,' Sally answered quietly. 'Inside I'm crying up a whole storm.'

The bounty hunter inhaled deeply. Then he nodded. 'Guess grief takes each of us different.'

Although he could not see her face he knew her expression had changed momentarily. Her words cut through the late afternoon air like a knife slitting a gizzard.

'I swear on my life I'm gonna kill them that done this, Iron Eyes. Kill them all and burn their filthy hides like they done to my kinfolk.'

Again Iron Eyes nodded in agreement. He knew the power the need for vengeance had on a person. It had driven him on for most of his life. It was a thirst which could never be quenched, though. He was about to turn when the enticing aroma of the cooking meat filled his flared nostrils again. 'Say, what you cooking there, Sally?' he asked in a low whisper.

'Squirrel. Head-shot squirrel,' she answered proudly with an exuberance he did not understand. 'Shot me a couple earlier when I was up in the hills hunting. Before I come back here to find my kin all gone.'

A wry smile etched across his horrific features, and he paused beside the small fire she had made. 'Squirrel?'

'Ya like squirrel?' She added more kindling to the flames over which she had suspended her game.

He nodded. 'Sure do, Squirrel Sally.'

'What you call me?' There was a boyish growl in her tone which made the bounty hunter step back.

'Nothing,' he lied.

'OK. Remember I still got me plenty of bullets left in that old carbine,' she warned.

Iron Eyes waved his hands as if in surrender.

'I ain't tasted squirrel in a whole heap of years, girl,' he admitted. His thin fingers pulled a twisted cigar from his shirt pocket and pushed it between his scarred lips. 'Sure smells good though. Smells mighty fine.'

'Can I have me a cigar?' Sally asked.

The tall man was not really surprised by her question. 'You smoke?'

'Sure enough. A pipe mostly.' Sally kept adding dry kindling to the fire that was roasting their supper. 'I run out of baccy though. Can I have me one of them cigars?'

The tall figure gave a long slow nod of his head. He pulled the twisted black cigar from his lips and held it at arm's length toward the young female.

'I reckon so. Here,' Iron Eyes said.

She snatched it from his bony fingers, rammed it into the corner of her mouth and then eagerly picked up a glowing branch from her fire. She held its hot tip to the end of the cigar and sucked in the smoke.

'Phew. That's good baccy.'

'Smoking ain't healthy for a young gal,' Iron Eyes told her as he searched his other pockets for a replacement cigar. 'Leastways, that's what I've heard.'

Her bright eyes looked at him. 'Reckon ya could be right. You sure look a real mess and no mistake. How long ya bin smoking these things?'

He paused, considered her words, then shook his head. This youngster seemed to have him figured out. 'You ain't partial to whiskey, I hope?'

'Nope.'

'Good,' he said firmly.

The bounty hunter knew that night was coming. His every sinew was telling him that there was only a couple of hours of sunlight left at most.

He then felt her hand catch the neck of his right boot. 'Are we gonna be heading on out after them killing bastards, Iron Eyes? After we has our vittles?'

For some reason which he could not fully understand he nodded. 'Yep. We'll head on out after them. With any luck they got bounty on them and—'

'I'll be ya eyes. I'll find their trail. Sit.' She patted

the ground beside her. Like an obedient hound he sat down where he heard her hand indicating.

'I gotta be honest with ya. I reckon we might be heading to our deaths, Squirrel,' he admitted. Blindly he stared at the fire and realized that he was now seeing even more light. 'I ain't the man I was a while back. Me being blind and all.'

Her soft lips kissed his cheek. 'Don't go fretting none, Iron Eyes. I'll look after ya.'

'I'm mighty grateful, Squirrel.' He grinned.

NINE

The diminishing sunlight meant nothing to Iron Eyes. He moved like a wounded mountain cat around the horse he had just saddled. His well-practised hands tossed his saddle-bags up over the blanket peering from beneath the ornate cantle and secured their leather laces. He could still feel the blood dripping on to his rugged battle-scarred features. His shirtfront was wet with the incessant flow of gore which had found its weathered cloth. A thought occurred to the forlorn figure. He wondered where his companion had disappeared to more than half an hour earlier.

Wherever it was she had gone to, Iron Eyes knew there had to be a damn good reason for it. Sally Cooke seemed to have a damn good reason for everything she did. His thin hand wiped the blood from his face.

For a man who prided himself on always travelling alone he perversely felt as though she ought to be at his side. She was a good shot and had eyes which were as keen as his once were. Squirrel Sally was a valuable asset for a man who was running mighty shy of valuable assets.

Iron Eyes gave out a muted laugh as he considered the events of the previous few hours. He had faced countless outlaws over the years and finished them all off sweetly and without a second thought or hint of guilt but it had taken a scrawny female to get the better of him.

The war drums inside his skull still pounded. Even a full belly had not managed to stop the maddening noise. He was still feeling the effects of his wounds. His back might have stopped bleeding beneath the ripped shirt and trail coat but he was feeling weakened from the loss of blood. He felt as though he were sinking into quicksand.

If he had been able to see properly this would never have happened, he silently told himself. His fingernails clawed at the broken cement cast on his head. It was stuck firm by months of sweat and blood.

Iron Eyes wanted to get rid of it but it had somehow become part of him. It had done its job and allowed his fractured skull to mend, but now it was just an annoyance. A damn annoyance. The haunting question returned to him again as it had done a thousand times.

Why was he still blind?

His head had healed and yet he was still blind.

Why?

He rested a hand on the stallion's neck, then listened to her bare feet as they approached him across the wide yard. There were other steps matching her own. Steps the bounty hunter knew were those of some small animal. A mule, or even a pony. His other senses were still compensating for the most priceless of them all. The one he needed the most.

'I got me a burro,' Sally announced as she reached his side. She was forced to look up towards his grim face. 'Them bandits didn't know about him. They stole all the other critters but they never even had themselves a clue about little Charlie here.'

'He sure don't sound too big. Is he up to carrying a full-grown female?' Iron Eyes sighed. His head hurt bad. He eased himself away from her and carefully edged back towards the saddle-bags. He opened the nearer of them and dragged one of his whiskey bottles free.

'Charlie can carry a full grown man,' she said.

Iron Eyes pulled the cork lifted the bottle to his lips. He took a long swallow and sighed again. 'Good old Charlie.'

'Ya look real awful, Iron Eyes,' Sally whispered. 'What's wrong?'

'I got me a real ornery pain inside my head, Squirrel,' he told her. 'And this blood is coming again. I heard tell that it ain't healthy to lose too much of the stuff.'

84

'Ya want me to take me a look at that wound of yours?' She touched his scarred face gently. 'I reckon that I can stop it bleeding.'

Iron Eyes smiled. 'I got me a gut feeling that you can do anything you set ya sights on, Squirrel. You kinda worry me in that respect. Never known anyone like ya. Are ya sure that ya can stop the bleeding?'

'Sure enough. Ya gotta learn how to do everything when ya lives out in the middle of nowhere.' She gave a nod, tied her reins to what was left of the hitching pole, then moved back to the man who towered over her small form. Her eyes stared at the bloodstain which had tricked down from the busted cement skullcap to the hem of his long coat. Fresh blood kept on adding to the mess. 'Hell. I sure seemed to have taken a mighty big chunk of ya head off with that bullet. Makes me almost regretful.'

'Almost?'

'Kinda.'

'Don't go fretting none. Most of the chunks of missing flesh was gone long before you shot at me.' There was a sound of weariness in Iron Eyes. He yawned, then felt her small hand take his and lead him away from the palomino and back to where he recognized the glow of her campfire. 'What ya intending on doing, Squirrel?'

'I ain't sure but ya must trust me.' She forced his long form down until he was seated close to the fire. 'You're in safe hands.'

'Yeah. The same hands that squeezed the trigger on that Winchester.' Iron Eyes took another swig from the bottle and felt it burning its way into his guts. 'I'm sure filled with a whole barn full of trust.'

'Ya ain't never gonna let that drop, are ya?' Sally slapped him around until he was seated exactly where she wanted him.

'Ain't a whole lot ya can do until ya get this cement Stetson off my damn head,' Iron Eyes muttered as he held the bottle to his lips.

She stood behind him. Even seated he was almost as tall as she was. She went up on to her toes and surveyed the top of his head curiously. 'How come you got this cement thing on ya head anyway? Ya hair has grown into it and its all stuck together.'

Silently, with his free hand, Iron Eyes pulled the Bowie knife from the neck of his boot. He raised it towards her. 'Here. Use this to cut it off. Ain't no use any more as it's all shot up.'

'Thank ya kindly.' Nervously Sally accepted the knife and looked at it. It was far heavier than she had imagined. It was also far sharper than any blade she had ever handled before. 'This what ya use when ya hunting?'

'Kinda,' Iron Eyes replied. 'It kills real good.'

Her hand began to shake. 'Y-yeah, I reckon it would.'

The bounty hunter took another mouthful of whiskey.

Carefully Sally began to ease the fragments of cement up away from the mane of long black hair. Blood covered her fingers from the graze that she could now see clearly. The honed edge of the blade separated the matted mane of hair from the grey encasement with an ease that terrified the female. It was like a hot knife going through butter.

Piece by piece was freed and then dropped on to the sandy ground beside the seated man, who kept sucking on the neck of his bottle. At last she had removed the last of the cement and thrown it away. She stared at the blood on the edge of the blade and her fingers. It was a gruesome sight.

The blood now seemed to be able to flow more freely as it pumped out of the exposed gash and then trailed along the length of his long hair before dripping over him like scarlet rain.

She gave a long sigh and pulled his head over until she was able to stare at the raw wound. 'Now let me get a better look at that graze, Iron Eyes.'

'Put the knife blade in the fire, Squirrel,' the bounty hunter said in a low authoritative drawl.

She paused. 'What?'

'Put the blade in the fire,' he repeated.

'Why?'

'It's gotta be red-hot, Squirrel.' Iron Eyes pointed at the flame, which he could vaguely make out. 'Ya have to feed that fire up a whole lot. Put some wood on it and get them flames high. The blade has to be

87

red-hot. Hear me?'

Sally walked around from behind him and then crouched down and looked into his emotionless face. 'I hear ya OK. Thing is I ain't sure why this knife gotta be red-hot.'

He remained quite still. 'To melt the skin and seal up the wound, that's why. Savvy?'

Shocked, she straightened up and felt her throat go dry. 'Ya want me to get this knife blade so hot it'll melt ya skin?'

'Yep,' he muttered between gulps of the whiskey he was steadily sipping.

'Hell!' Sally blinked hard, then grabbed the bottle from his hand and took a long swig herself. She coughed as the flames inside her gullet confirmed the strength of his hard liquor. After catching her breath she forced the bottle back into her seated companion's grasp. 'Are you loco? Ya want me to put a red-hot lump of steel on ya head?'

Iron Eyes moved his head until it was turned directly towards her shocked and frightened face. 'I don't want ya to do it but there ain't no other way to stop it bleeding. It has to be burned.'

'I – I could sew it up.' Sally was desperately trying to find another way of achieving what he desired. Something less revolting. She glanced over her shoulder at the charred remnants of what had once been her family home and then realized that every-thing had gone up in flames, her mother's sewing kit being just one of them. 'Hell.'

He touched her leg and drew her attention.

'What?' Sally snapped as she stared at the huge knife still in her shaking hand. 'Ya got something else in mind for me to do? Like me maybe cutting off ya leg or the like? I can't go putting no red-hot knife on ya head.'

'Sure ya can.' He sounded as though he actually believed his words. 'If anyone can melt old Iron Eyes's head it's Squirrel Sally.'

'Ya hair might catch fire,' Sally ventured.

'Wouldn't be the first time.' He smiled.

'Ya might die of shock.'

'That'll be the day.'

Sally now sounded frantic. 'B-but this ain't right.'

'Just do it,' he insisted.

'It'll hurt.'

He looked back at the fire. 'Everything in life hurts, Squirrel. The hurt only stops when you're dead.'

Reluctantly she began to feed the fire with everything she could lay her hands on. Within moments it was raging before them. Sally then bent over and pushed the long wide blade into the heart of the fire. She rose back to her full five feet and rested a hand on his shoulder. She felt the drops of blood touching the back of her hand.

Suddenly she knew he was right. It was the only sure way to stop the wound from bleeding.

89

'H-how long does it take for the blade to get hot enough, Iron Eyes?' Sally asked nervously.

He took another swallow of the fiery whiskey.

'Not long.'

'Oh hell.' She grabbed the bottle again and took another gulp. It tasted no less powerful than the first swig. She coughed and gave it back to him. 'How can ya drink that stuff?'

He inhaled deeply.

'Reckon it's ready,' Iron Eyes said.

'How can ya tell?' Sally squeezed his shoulder. 'Ya can't see it. How can ya tell it's hot enough already?'

'I just know.'

TEN

The haunting sound of howling coyotes off in the distance echoed all around the yard. Their wailing screams were familiar to the thin man who had heard their plaintive calls for his entire life. They were baying at the moon and the stars as they had done since time itself had begun. They were dangerous creatures when hungry but none had ever dared venture close to the man who carried the scent of all his kills with him wherever he went. It might have been a primitive respect or just plain fear but coyotes, like most other living things, remained well out of range when Iron Eyes was close.

His practised fingers had secured the cinch straps and then lowered the fender twenty or more minutes earlier. He had filled his canteens and grained the tall stallion and ensured that his trusty Navy Colts were fully loaded and ready for action, but now all he could do was sit and wait for his tiny companion to

91

awaken. The campfire still had the scent of the food they had eaten wafting in its smoke.

It was now quite dark. Iron Eyes could feel the cold night air starting to gnaw its way into his bones as he continued to suck the last of the amber liquor from the bottle in his left hand. The smell of his smouldering scalp still filled his flared nostrils. The flames of the fire were at last starting to ebb.

His long bony fingers reached up and carefully touched his still tender scalp. She had done her job, he thought. Done it well for a youngster who had never done anything like that before.

Iron Eyes turned his head to face the spot where he had heard her fall only a few seconds after pressing the hot blade of his knife against the bloody rip in his scalp. He gave out a grunting laugh and reached out until his searching fingers came across her small bare feet.

She was still there, still holding on to the knife which she had used to brand the flesh together as he had ordered her to do.

Not many females of any age would have had the guts to do that, he told himself. He shook her feet hard and heard her snort. Iron Eyes knew that it was getting colder and they had to start travelling before the frost started to eat into them.

'You ever gonna wake up, Squirrel?' he grumbled for the umpteenth time. 'I'm getting damn cold sitting here waiting for you to stir, gal.'

He felt her feet pull away from his skeletal fingers as she rolled over on to her belly. She was groaning the way all young females do when greeted with a face full of dirt.

'W-what?' Sally mumbled and spat.

'Howdy.' Iron Eyes greeted her as he listened to her efforts to rise off the ground. 'I said it's time we headed on out from here.'

'What happened?' she asked.

'Ya fainted.'

She scrambled up on to all fours, crawled to his side and rested her head on his thin leg.

'I did not faint,' she insisted.

'I reckon it was the smell.' He nodded and then placed a hand on her soft hair.

She glanced up at him. His face seemed no less horrific even in the dim light of the dying campfire. Yet she was totally unafraid. It was as though she saw something in the bounty hunter that no one else had ever perceived. 'Shut up. I didn't faint. I ain't no fancy weak-legged female, all blushes and war paint.'

He stroked her head as she rested it on his leg. 'Ain't no shame in fainting. I seen grown men drop down in a trembling heap when something scared them good enough.'

'I did not faint. It was that rotgut. It made me giddy.' She suddenly realized she still had his Bowie knife in her hand. Slowly she returned it to his boot.

'Must be real dark now.' Iron Eyes tossed the

empty bottle away. 'The night critters are all in full voice.'

Sally raised her head and listened. She had not noticed it herself but the area was alive with the sounds of living things all heralding the darkness.

'I never ever heard that before,' she remarked. 'I can hear a million bugs and coyotes and—'

'I don't like wild critters. Let's head on out.' Iron Eyes carefully eased his tortured frame up until he attained his full height. 'Snakes is the worst. Them things come out at night and bite ya.'

Sally used him to help her get back up on to her feet and hung on his lean frame as though it were a crutch. 'Are ya telling me that you're scared of snakes and bugs and the like?'

He paused for a moment and thought about the question as she took hold of his arm.

'Yep,' he admitted.

She was laughing out loud all the way back to the horse and her burro. Iron Eyes liked the sound.

Upon reaching the animals the tall man made his way round the stallion until he reached the other saddle-bag and opened it. He reached inside it and pulled out a long bloodstained frock-coat that he had taken from a dead undertaker months earlier.

'Here.' Iron Eyes tossed it over the saddle to where he could still hear her giggling at his expense. 'This'll keep ya warm.'

Sally held the coat in her hands. Even the eerie

light of the moon and stars could not disguise the bloodstains and bullet holes in the garment. 'Where'd ya get this old thing?'

'Off an undertaker.' Iron Eyes made his way carefully round the stallion.

'Didn't he want it no more?'

A wicked grin filled the scarred face of the tall man as he recollected the incident. 'Nope. He was dead, so I figured that it would serve me better than him.'

'D-did you kill him?' Sally managed to ask.

'Hell no. I didn't kill him,' the bounty hunter answered. 'But I sure killed the varmints that did though, gal. Killed 'em all real good and permanent.'

She absorbed his words, then eased the coat on to her small frame. It almost reached the ground and she had to roll up its sleeve cuffs to find her hands.

'It's nice and warm,' she said as though she were wearing the most fashionable of jackets and not a coat still bearing the bullet holes which had killed its original owner. 'I never had me a real coat before.'

'It'll keep the frost out of ya bones,' Iron Eyes said bluntly. 'C'mon. We got some riding to do.'

She unhitched the burro's crude reins and pulled the small animal away from its far bigger cousin.

'How's them war drums in ya head, Iron Eyes?'

'A whole heap better, gal. Them pesky Apaches must have gotten themselves plumb tuckered.' He listened to her mounting her bareback burro before his hands found his reins and teased them free of the hitching pole. His keen hearing heard her priming her Winchester. He reached up, grabbed his saddle horn, stepped into the stirrup and dragged his thin body up on to the high-shouldered stallion in one fluid action. 'Ya done a real fine job on my head, gal. I'm much obliged.'

Sally said nothing but he knew she was smiling.

The bounty hunter looked up and realized that he could see the moon with one eye at least. It was not in focus but he could see it. Suddenly Iron Eyes felt a new confidence flowing through him. Maybe this time his sight would return permanently, he thought.

'You reckon ya know which way we gotta head, Squirrel?' Iron Eyes asked her.

'Sure enough. I know which way them rustling bastards went with our herd of white faces, Iron Eyes,' Sally answered, turning the small burro around and tapping its sides with her heels. 'They carved up a mighty deep trail.'

He gave a satisfied nod of his head and tossed his reins down into her hands. Sally wrapped the long leathers around her wrist and balanced her Winchester across her lap.

'Then lead the way, Squirrel.' Iron Eyes gestured before looking back up at the moon. His left eye was gradually becoming able to focus upon it.

The moonlight cast its chilling bluish illumination

96

over the small burro as it led the large stallion away from the devastated yard. Their riders riding astride their animals could not have been more different from one another.

It was a strange sight, but there was no one to witness it.

A salvo of gunfire announced the arrival of the four horsemen as they thundered into El Remo. Everyone knew when Mexican Pete and his handful of ruthless cronies were back in town. Especially when their pockets were bulging with the spoils of their ill-gotten gains. Their roaring six-shooters blasted up into the star-filled sky as the lethal riders carved a route towards the centre of El Remo. Pete wanted them all to know that the town's most notorious son had returned triumphantly from yet another profitable adventure.

The smell of the coal-tar lanterns that lit the lawless town could not overcome the putrid aroma which blanketed El Remo. Yet it seemed as if none of the people who filled its every building and street noticed anything unusual. They had grown used to the stench that might have repelled more sensitive nostrils.

Mexican Pete had returned with only three of his raiding band beside him. The others had taken their pay and fled to the nearest watering hole, close to where Pete had sold the herd of rustled steers. But that was not good enough for the bandit who thrived on his fame within El Remo. Pete was a large fish in a very small pond. He knew few would ever challenge him in the sprawling settlement perched upon the ragged cliff top. Here he was a king amongst knaves. Elsewhere he was just another sweat-soaked bandit.

The four horsemen had blasted off all of their ammunition by the time they reached the large cantina. The stagecoach and its six-horse team were exactly where Burr had abandoned them. The bandits drew rein and allowed their mounts to drink from the water troughs as they speedily reloaded their arsenal of smoking firearms. As the bullets were pushed into the hot chambers Mexican Pete and his followers noticed the dead man lying at the foot of the steps, where he had fallen from the boardwalk. The bandit leader stared down at the body of the large Mexican with more than a hint of amusement.

'Is that who I think it is, *amigos?*'

The three others grunted.

No one had bothered to remove the dead body even though it was now three hours since Mason Burr had killed the man. The amber lights which cascaded from the busy cantina flickered and danced across the body. It had been stripped of its boots and six-shooter but otherwise was exactly as it had been when the trio of expertly placed bullets had ended its futile existence.

Mexican Pete was first to reload his guns and dismount. He looped his reins around the neck of the water pump beside the hitching pole and bent over to get a better look at the already festering corpse.

A wide smile revealed his golden front teeth. He began to laugh as Harper, Pedro and One-eared Sanchez dropped down to the ground behind him.

'Hey, look, boys.' Pete laughed as he pointed a finger at the fly-covered body. 'I think this is Fernando.'

Ty Harper walked up and kicked the body so hard it went over on to its back. A cloud of flies rose and then returned to their feast. The dead face still had the same confused expression on it as when life had left it.

'Yep. It's Fernando OK.' Harper grunted. He rubbed the back of his neck and secured his horse to the rail, next to Pete's.

'He must have upset someone.' Pedro shrugged as he stared down at the group of bullet holes set between the crossed ammunition belts. 'Whoever did this was a good shot, Pete.'

The town had come to life as soon as the sun had set and the lanterns had been lit. Scores of people were still passing in all directions as the bandit leader turned to face the canteen. He grabbed one of the men who was ambling aimlessly past him. He shook the figure and then pushed his face up close to that of the startled drunk.

'Who killed Fernando?' he growled threateningly.

The question seemed to confuse further the already drink-hazed man. He blinked hard and gazed down at the body. 'Hell. I never noticed that before.'

'Before what?' Sanchez asked over Pete's shoulder.

'Before I was drunk,' the man explained.

Mexican Pete pushed the man aside and placed a boot on the bottom step of the cantina. Then he heard muted laughter coming from above them. Removing his sombrero Pete looked up and cast his hungry eyes on two females who were allowing their assets to overflow from their dresses.

'Did you see who killed this fool, ladies?' Pete called up.

One of the females gave a nod. 'A dude. The dude who brung that coach into town.'

Pete turned to the others. 'What is a dude?'

Ty Harper stepped next to his leader and smiled at the well-endowed pair. 'Where did he go?'

She pointed over the balcony rail at the cantina's front door. 'In there. He's not come out since.'

'This dude got a handle?' Harper asked.

'Mason Burr,' the other female chimed in. 'He was asking about ya, Pete. Fernando wouldn't let him come into the cantina and the dude just got a tad ornery.'

Mexican Pete leaned closer to Harper and the other two bandits closed in beside them.

'Who is this Mason Burr?'

Harper pushed his Stetson off his brow. 'Whoever he is he sure can shoot.'

'He was asking for ya by name, Pete,' Sanchez remarked. 'He must know of you even if you have never heard of him.'

'And he wants you, Pete.' Pedro gulped.

Mexican Pete pulled both his guns from their holsters and gritted his golden teeth. 'C'mon. Let's go find this dude. Let's see what he wants of Mexican Pete.'

The four men strode up to the boardwalk, paused to cock their weapons, then entered.

The cantina fell silent.

ELEVEN

The four bandits burst into the busy cantina fast and furious and made sure that every living soul within its walls knew of their arrival. Yet all the gunplay was meant to frighten only one man amid a sea of so many other men. Mexican Pete and his three hired vermin wanted the mysterious Mason Burr to know that not all the men in El Remo were as easily killed as the one he had left rotting on the cantina steps. Their guns blazed bullets in all directions as the quartet cut a wide swath between the terrified cantina patrons. There must have been a hundred souls inside the cantina but by the time the bandits had unleashed a score of bullets into its walls and ceiling only one remained seated and seemingly unimpressed.

Burr looked up from his table. It amused him that so many people were trying to press themselves up against the tobacco-stained wallpaper. A sly smile etched his face as he silently surveyed the four men.

'Who looks for Mexican Pete?' the leader of the outlaws shouted. Then he noticed Burr. 'Is it you?'

'Indeed it is, friend.' Mason Burr remained seated at the round card table, pondering over his glass and bottle of whiskey. The trickster knew that the man he sought out had arrived. 'Join me in a glass of whiskey.'

The surprised bandits made their way through the smoke-filled room towards him. Most men might have been alarmed by the sight of so many guns. Especially when it was clear that every one of those weapons was aimed at him. Yet unlike every other person inside the cantina Mason Burr was totally unafraid.

The men loomed over the table. Smoke billowed from their gun barrels but Burr remained apparently unimpressed. He tilted his head back, then narrowed his eyes as he studied the men. He smiled and pointed at the empty chairs around his table.

'Sit down, Pete,' Burr said in a low dry tone.

Mexican Pete raised an eyebrow and glanced at each of his three men in turn before returning his curious eyes to the man seated before them.

'You know who I am, *señor*?'

'Everyone knows of Mexican Pete.' Burr flattered his prey with a well-rehearsed look. 'You are famous in at least a dozen territories.'

'I am?' A smile of golden teeth flashed down at the

man who was far more deadly than any of them realized. Pete dragged a chair away from the table and lowered himself upon it. He kept his guns cocked and trained upon the man in the dusty suit. 'So you are Mason Burr.'

'Indeed.' Burr nodded. 'You have heard of me?'

'Nope,' Pete answered quickly. 'A whore told me ya name.'

Burr smiled as wide as the man opposite him. 'You are the man I have travelled a hundred miles to find, Pete. The only man I consider worthy of my expert guidance.'

Mexican Pete sucked in his cheeks. 'You come all that way to find me? Why? Explain.'

'Business.' Burr reached out, took hold of his whiskey bottle and filled the glass. 'I have a business deal for you which I think will make us both rich. Very rich.'

The three other men sat down around their leader. They were all watching Pete as he tried to understand the words he had just heard.

'How rich?'

'Very.'

'Don't trust him, Pete,' Harper advised. 'I seen his breed before, up north. He'll steal the filling out of ya teeth and then send ya a bill.'

'Kill him, Pete.' Sanchez nodded firmly.

Mason Burr glanced at Pedro and awaited his comments. Pedro just shrugged.

Mexican Pete released the hammers on his guns and then holstered them both. He leaned forward, rested both elbows on the table and glared at Burr hard. 'Business?'

'Very profitable business.' Burr sipped at his whiskey and looked at the three men flanking Pete. 'Help yourselves to the whiskey, boys.'

Mexican Pete snapped the fingers of his left hand until he knew he had Burr's full attention.

'Listen, *amigo.* I rustle and kill,' Pete said. 'This is my business. How can you offer me something to make me rich? I do not understand.'

Burr was like a man with a fishing rod seated on a riverbank awaiting a bite. He knew when the hook had been taken by his intended target. Pete had swallowed the hook and it was now time to haul him in.

Burr lowered his glass from his lips. 'What would you say if I had a way for you and your friends to make a thousand times more money than you have ever seen?'

'Who do we have to kill?' Pete wondered aloud.

'No one.' Burr smiled.

'Impossible,' Harper snapped, hitting the table top with a fist. 'Ain't no way folks can make that kinda money without killing being involved. Don't trust him, Pete. He's up to something.'

'Something to make you all rich,' Mason Burr bravely interrupted. 'Unless you are afraid of making enough money to retire with, boys.'

One-eared Sanchez rubbed the side of his head where he had once had an ear. 'How is this possible? I do not understand.'

'Explain,' Mexican Pete demanded.

Harper eased back on his chair and stared at Burr. He continued to watch the man silently.

Mason Burr rose to his feet and placed the empty glass down on the baize. He smiled, then picked up his hat and bag and began to move away from the table. Mexican Pete jumped to his feet.

'Where are you going, *amigo*?'

Burr sighed and looked at the staircase. 'To my room. I need to freshen up.'

Pete moved around the table and blocked the path of the well-dressed man. 'No. You cannot go now. You have not explained how I can become richer than I ever dreamed possible.'

Both men paused a mere three feet from the other.

'Later.' Burr lowered his head and stared with deadly cold eyes at the bandit. 'I have ladies to entertain.'

Pete recalled how fast this man must have been with his hidden six-shooter. He drew a breath and stepped out of Burr's way. He felt his blood run ice-cold and gave a sheepish nod.

'We shall be waiting for you to return, my friend.'

Burr looked at them all in turn. 'Later.'

Mexican Pete sat down again next to his men, and

they all watched Burr ascend the flight of steps to the landing. There were at least three females awaiting Burr. They wrapped themselves around him and led him to a room.

Pete signalled to the barman. 'Tequilas. Four bottles.'

'That man is dangerous, Pete,' Harper said. He grabbed the whiskey bottle and took a long swallow from it. 'I reckon he might be some kinda bounty hunter. Fancy, but still out to get the reward money on our heads north of the border.'

'I know,' Pete agreed.

'He is dishonest I think,' Pedro announced.

The others all looked at their companion. Sanchez shook his head and accepted the bottle from Harper. 'I think Pedro has forgotten that we are also dishonest.'

'I reckon that dude will be the death of us all,' Ty Harper murmured. 'Gotta be a bounty hunter. Gotta be.'

Mexican Pete grinned widely. His gold teeth flashed in the lanternlight. 'No, *amigo*. You are wrong about him being the death of us. It shall be I who bring death to him when I have learned what his plan is. Mason Burr thinks he is smart. I shall make sure that he dies thinking that.'

The mutual laughter encircled the table.

TWELVE

Like a mechanical heart beating, the wall clock inside the cantina seemed to be the only sound any of the occupants could hear. Its relentless ticking echoed off the stained walls in a constant reminder of what might happen at any moment. Lanternlight glanced off the barrels of the numerous guns which were held in unsettled gloved hands. The darkest of souls had gathered inside the cantina as rumours had quickly spread like wildfire amongst the handful of men who ruled the bandit stronghold. Rumours that the stranger named Mason Burr was offering Mexican Pete the opportunity of making a fortune to outstrip all other fortunes. Of all the outlaw and bandit leaders apart from Mexican Pete, there were just three who were just as dangerous and could muster a small army of dead-shot guns at the drop of a hat.

Until now they had all waged war against one

another, to try and keep one step ahead of the competition, and to secure even more of El Remo's numerous spoils. But now with the mere hint of there being a fortune to be made the three gang leaders had gathered with some of their troops, like bears to a honeypot, in the very same place.

It had never happened before and it would probably never happen again. A mixture of curiosity and greed had brought about the seemingly impossible. Using his as yet unchallenged authority Mason Burr had achieved the impossible.

Without even having to be in the same room Burr had set the traps and allowed the vermin to throw themselves upon them in his absence.

It was an unnerving sight even for the most fool-hardy and daredevilish of souls. The four main groups took up their positions in separate corners of the cantina with rifles and guns cocked in readiness for action.

Jed Sumner, Pancho Valez and Sven Anderson were as different as chalk is from cheese but they were all cast from the same corrupt mould. They controlled sections of the sprawling town, and when those sections overlapped there was only one result. Guns would be hot and spewing lead plentifully. Each of the gang leaders had murdered their way to the top of his individual tree. They were all rich by any standards and yet, as with all those who have more than they actually require, they wanted more.

109

None of the cantina regulars had ever witnessed all of the gangs in one place at the same time before and it frightened most into leaving the drinking hole. For even a drunken fool does not wish to be in the same room as a stick of dynamite when it explodes. Each of these villainous men was as dangerous as any high explosive. They killed for money. For pleasure.

Mexican Pete was probably as wealthy as any of the men he and his three henchmen studied from behind their tequilas bottles but, unlike them, Pete was not self-deluded enough to pretend he was anything else than what he appeared to be.

And he was a heartless killer and thief.

There was tension growing inside the cantina as the men drank their fill of hard liquor and watched one another in readiness for the bullets to begin flying. Eyes darted from one group to another. The smell of sweat began to overwhelm the cantina's other pungent odours.

And the wall clock kept on ticking.

Yet for all the tension there was also a curiosity which kept them from being the first to start the inevitable killing. They all wanted to know one thing: when would Mason Burr return down to the belly of the drinking hole to elaborate on his plan.

When would Burr walk back down those damn stairs?

It seemed as though there were invisible fences

110

keeping the four gangs apart. All of them seemed to have found a place where their backs were against a wall and they had full uninterrupted views of the entire interior of the drinking hole.

The clock kept on ticking.

Anderson had seated himself in the middle of his five hired guns and was drinking slowly as he watched the others like a hawk. Directly across from Anderson the oldest of the outlaw leaders, Jed Sumner, had also found a chair which suited his wide girth and was also drinking whilst flanked by at least ten of his best men.

Pancho Valez had brought only two of his top guns with him and was feeling anxious about the situation. He sat in a corner where the light of the cantina's numerous lanterns could not find him. A spot where he prayed bullets would also not find him.

Only Mexican Pete remained out in the open, with his trio of men surrounding him at the same card table that Burr had vacated nearly an hour earlier. They knew that when the shooting started there would be no safe place in the cantina; one place was as good or as bad as the next.

Harper kept both his guns on the green baize table with his fingers curled in their trigger guards. He watched the other groups like a fox watches its prey, carefully and without any sign of emotion.

'I think we should go, Pete,' Pedro said. 'I am tired.'

111

Pete glanced at the yawning bandit. 'You stay until I say we go. Savvy, *amigo*?'

Pedro nodded. '*Sí.*'

One-eared Sanchez had sat with his back to the rest of the cantina for that same long hour. He eventually turned his chair around and looked directly at the other groups of men, who all seemed to have more firepower than was needed.

'This is bad,' Sanchez said. 'I did not think there were that many of the bastards here, Pete. We are outgunned.'

Mexican Pete patted Sanchez's face. 'They will not use their weapons. They are here because of our friend. They want to know the plan, just as we do.'

'We have no friend,' Sanchez argued.

'I mean Burr, idiot,' Pete whispered through his gold teeth. 'Unlike you, this cantina has many ears. When Burr was bragging to us I think the word spread around to the other gangs, and they wish to steal our booty. They wish Burr to make them rich and not us.'

'Does this mean we ain't gonna kill Burr?' Pedro yawned and stretched his arms. 'I was looking forward to killing him.'

'I still don't trust the varmint,' Harper chipped in.

Pedro poured himself another glassful of the clear liquor and downed it in one throw. 'Are we going to kill him or not?'

Mexican Pete was about to reply when he heard

the door at the top of the stairs open. His eyes screwed up, and he and every other man inside the cantina focused upon Burr as he came back on to the landing. The satisfied sound of well-paid whores bidding farewell to their latest patron washed down over the anxious onlookers.

'There he is, *amigos*.' Pete pointed. 'He is satisfied and is coming back down to speak to us. Now we shall discover what this fancy *hombre* has planned. Now we shall find out how we will all get rich.'

Ty Harper chewed on a tobacco plug, then spat at the floor. 'He ain't gonna like the fact that Sumner and the other high hats are all here, Pete. He might figure we bin talking to the bastards.'

Mexican Pete gave a sly glance over his shoulder at the others, who watched Burr even more closely than he had done himself. 'I think you might be right, *amigo*.'

'Not that I believed one single word that fancy dude said,' Harper added thoughtfully.

'I want to kill him,' Pedro snarled, filling his glass again. 'He is too clean.'

Mexican Pete removed his sombrero briefly and swatted the bandit as if he were a fly. 'Silence. I shall tell you when to kill him. You keep watching the *hombres* behind us. They are hungry, *amigo*. Hungry to kill us.'

Mason Burr adjusted his hat, gripped his bag firmly in his left hand and began the slow descent into the heart of the cantina. With each step he watched the men inside the room and noted with brilliant instinct who their paymasters were. A wry smile filled his face.

The wall clock began to chime eleven.

'Come into my parlour. . .' he whispered.

THIRTEEN

The spider had taken only an hour to draw each of the four outlaw leaders into his alluring web. They had become entangled in it and no matter how much they might have fought against it they were all doomed to failure. For Mason Burr had the advantage over them all. He knew he was dishonest, but they, like so many other men on either side of the law, could not admit the truth even to themselves.

They were greedy and that was their weakness, the chink in their otherwise impenetrable armour. Burr had always known that you cannot trick honest men but these were far from honest men. Like a card-sharp who could deal himself a winning hand, the deadly trickster used words to bend the will of those he wished to fleece. Years of well-rehearsed deception had brought them exactly where he had wanted to get them.

At his mercy.

They were almost fighting one another to part with their life savings for the promise of riches to come. No honest person would have ever fallen for the tricks employed by Mason Burr. Yet, as always, he knew he was dealing with people who did not even knew what the word meant.

For Burr it was just another job, one he had been planning for months. The ultimate trick. To take hardened bandits for everything they had and then, when the moment was right, kill any of them who got in his way.

To Sumner, Valez, Anderson and Mexican Pete it was the promise of something for nothing. The allure of the forbidden fruits he had convinced them they would wallow in. They had fallen for his silky delivery of each well-considered word.

The wall clock let them know it was midnight.

The smiles of thieves who think that they have managed to steal something from the unwary had once again been their downfall. To Burr it mattered little who his victims were. The confidence trick was just a means to an end. Burr had more than enough money but he knew the demon inside him could never be satisfied.

He had to kill. Kill again and again.

It was only the kill he craved nowadays. He had become addicted to the ultimate thrill. His eyes darted around the table at their faces. Their greedy faces. Which one would he kill, he asked himself?

116

Why not attempt to kill more than one?

He smiled the smile of an innocent as he surveyed them arguing. There was no hint of the lurid thoughts which filled his depraved mind. He would be merciless in his execution of not only the deal but those he intended to slaughter. These men were no different from all the others he had lured into his deadly web.

They deserved to die. They craved something for nothing. What they would get was a stark reminder that everything has a price.

A bloody price.

There was a sickening expression of satisfaction on the faces of all of the four men who sat around the card table. Each thought that he had somehow managed to get the better of the others. Each considered that what he had agreed to was a form of stealing but one which ordinary folks use each and every day. Banks sell worthless shares to those who fall for the promise of profits for nothing. A thousand excuses and the protective warmth of the law to make their stealing legal somehow seemed perfectly normal to the men who had agreed to give all of their money to the trickster who sat with handfuls of fake bonds and share certificates in his hands.

The San Angelo Mining Company sounded real enough to the men who were more used to stealing gold than investing in the companies who mined it, but the documents were like Burr himself.

117

A fistful of phoney paper.

Like the others gathered around the table, Mexican Pete had drooled when he had listened to the words which had spewed non-stop from Burr. The bandit had never imagined that there was a fortune waiting to be had by simply buying shares and allowing others to do all the hard work.

Mexican Pete did not know it but his first instinct had been correct. It was too good to be true.

'So it's agreed?' Burr asked them in his most honest of voices. 'The men willing to buy all of these shares will own fifty-one per cent of the company.'

Anderson looked at his fellow competitors. 'How long before we make this fortune, Burr?'

Mason Burr frowned. 'Within thirty days of registration, my friend.'

Sumner leaned over the table and stared at the certificates spread out before them. 'Ya say they struck a mother lode of gold in San Angelo, Burr?'

Mason Burr slowly nodded. 'Indeed. My brother is the chief engineer in charge of the mining there. He tells me that they have struck gold. It is a small seam, but he has discovered a far larger one which he has not even notified his employers of yet. This is why the share price is so low. Once the announcement is made of the larger strike the price of these shares will go through the roof. You will become millionaires when you sell them.'

Now all of the men were drooling.

'Thirty days.' Valez repeated the words. 'I like this very much.'

'How much will it cost to buy all of the shares you have there, Burr?' Anderson asked, licking his lips.

'A mere ten thousand dollars,' Burr replied without looking at any of them. 'I have to make a profit for my brother and myself.'

'What will they be worth after the announce-ment?' Sumner eagerly enquired.

'A thousand times that,' Burr answered. 'But you understand that as a registered broker I shall have to have the cash to deposit into the bank at El Paso within a week so that the deal is certified.'

The men went into instant conference.

Sumner held out a hand to Burr. 'My new partners and I will have ten thousand dollars in cash and coin on this table before noon, Burr.'

'Excellent.'

The clock was still ticking.

Mason Burr was still smiling. He could almost taste the blood he knew he would soon be spilling.

The richest men in El Remo all stood and led their respective armies out into the wide street. All except Mexican Pete, who remained sitting and chewing on a cigar as he watched Burr travel back up to his room carrying his bag. Pete was also smiling as Pedro resumed his seat next to his leader.

'I did not understand any of the talk, Pete,' Pedro admitted.

119

'The words meant nothing, *amigo*,' Mexican Pete told him as he heard the whores greeting the return of their client on the high landing. 'It is the money which sings to me.'

Pedro then saw Ty Harper and One-eared Sanchez enter the cantina through a curtain of beads at the rear of the wide room.

'Where they bin?' Pedro asked.

Pete stood up and walked through the cigar smoke towards his two favoured gunmen. He rested an elbow on the wet bar counter as both Harper and Sanchez reached his side.

'We done it, Pete.' Harper grinned.

'Twenty of our best men,' Sanchez added. 'They all accepted the golden eagles and are waiting in the street.'

'Good.' Pete grinned. 'I have waited years to get those stinking *hombres* in one place together to kill them.'

Pedro rose again from the chair by the table and staggered sleepily to the three others. 'What is going on?'

Mexican Pete pulled a match from his pocket, ran it up the side of his pants leg, then stared at its glowing flame as though it were a crystal ball.

'This is Anderson, Valez and Sumner and all of their fat men.' Pete grinned with golden teeth at the flickering flame. He then blew at the flame and it was extinguished in a sad puff of smoke. '*Adios, amigos.*'

Suddenly the street erupted into battle. No thunderstorm could have been so deafening. Rifles and six-shooters were blazing their deadly fury out in the street as Pete's rivals were caught in a well-planned crossfire. Every eye inside the cantina was drawn to the windows and door as venomous flashes cut through the air beyond their adobe walls. The sound of screams mixed with shots filled their ears.

Even though riddled with countless bullets Sven Anderson somehow managed to drag himself back to the cantina where he had thought the thick adobe walls might offer him some protection. He took three faltering steps into the drinking hole when he saw the smiling face of Mexican Pete.

'P-Pete?' Anderson gasped.

Pete drew and fired both his guns. Anderson was lifted off the floor and thrown back out into the street. Pete holstered both weapons as quickly as he had drawn them.

'By the sound of it I reckon we done picked the right boys, Pete.' Harper grinned.

There was no argument. Mexican Pete took hold of the nearest bottle and began to pour himself a long drink just as he heard the door on the landing abruptly reopen. Pete glanced up and saw the startled Burr standing with his pants in disarray.

'What's happening?' Burr yelled down at Pete and his three cohorts. 'What's happening, Pete?'

Mexican Pete raised his glass to Burr. 'A little

change of plan, *amigo*. You did not fool me like ya fooled them.'

'What?' Mason Burr gripped the railing at the top of the stairs. His knuckles went white as he listened to the fighting outside in the street growing more intense with every tick of the cantina wall clock.

Pete swallowed the entire contents of the glass, then lowered it as his eyes burned up at Mason Burr. 'You are a sweet-talking man, *señor*. But Mexican Pete has heard many sweet-talking men in his time.'

Suddenly realizing that his plan was melting with every shot he heard being fired out in the street Burr desperately went for the gun hanging precariously in its shoulder holster. He fumbled for the gun grip and, after some moments, managed to draw the weapon. Burr aimed it at Mexican Pete.

'Then die,' Burr screamed.

It was too late though.

Ty Harper drew and fanned his hammer twice before Burr had even managed to cock his firearm. The bullets hit their target high under the trickster's chin. Burr coughed as blood splattered from his throat. He staggered, then stumbled over the top step. He came crashing head over heels down the flight of stairs, leaving a trail of gore in his wake until he slid to where all four bandits were standing.

The arrogant Mason Burr had tasted blood again. Sadly for him it was his own.

The startled Pedro gripped his leader's arm. 'But

what of the fortune, Pete? He said he would make us all richer than we could ever dream. Now Burr is dead all is lost.'

Pete kicked the head at his feet and then spat at it. 'You are wrong, Pedro. He has made us rich.'

'He has?' Sanchez queried. 'How?'

The shooting outside stopped. A deathly silence filled the cantina as one by one the men Harper had hired began to file into the drinking hole with their smoking weapons in their hands. A collective nod from each of them to their leader made Mexican Pete roar with laughter.

The other gang leaders were now nothing more than a memory.

Pete wrapped his arms around the shoulders of Sanchez and Pedro and looked up at the rafters.

'What do we need with stinking paper fortunes? We are now rich, *amigos*. Richer than we ever thought possible. For we now own the whole town. We own El Remo.'

FOURTEEN

The small burro and its mistress had led the palomino stallion throughout the bone-biting hours of darkness deep into the untamed Mexican wastelands. Rolling dunes glistened with frost beneath the bright yellow moon and a myriad stars lent their brilliance to the further reaches of the sky. This was a lonely land during the day but at night it became almost mystical. Sally's keen eyes had enabled them to follow the trail left by her family's herd of white-faced cattle for nearly twenty miles until the moon and stars had faded, to be replaced by the blinding rays of the rising sun.

Both horse and burro stopped as the dazzling light spread towards them across the land like a tidal wave of sheer brilliance. The stallion shied as it felt the sudden heat hit it. Sally Cooke turned her small burro round and looked up at the grim-faced bounty hunter, who sat like a deathly scarecrow atop his magnificent palomino.

Iron Eyes might have been a statue carved from granite for all the life he displayed. There was no sign of life in his horrific form. He just sat bathed in the rays of sun, looking like a totem carving.

For what seemed an eternity Sally just stared at him as the full glare of the sun illuminated his every bloodcurdling feature. He had told her during their long ride that there were many men who thought that he was a ghost bent on revenge. A dead man who was too ornery to admit he was no longer alive. Seeing him now awash in the almost satanic rays, she knew why those stories had taken root. Few men could have presented a more frightening spectacle whether dead or alive.

Yet for all his horrific appearance she was still quite unafraid of the man of whom, in some ways, she had proved to be the equal. For some reason that she could not herself understand, she believed that this man of all men had the power to help her wreak her vengeance.

Iron Eyes still did not move. Did not even blink.

He sat propped in his high saddle allowing the warmth of the new day to burn the cold out of his bones.

'Ya looks mighty ugly this morning, Iron Eyes,' Sally told him as she dropped from the back of her burro and adjusted the ill-fitting frock-coat. 'Ugly ain't even a big enough word to tell folks how bad ya look.'

He did not reply. He simple sat staring straight into the light of the low sun as it sat just above the nearest dune, trying to climb up into the blue sky.

'Ya gonna feed and water that horse of yours?' she added as she led the small burro up to the stallion's nose. 'Well? Is ya or is ya ain't?'

Iron Eyes continued to look straight ahead.

'Is ya asleep? Is ya dead?' Sally tied her crude reins to the stallion's bridle and walked towards the canteens and saddle-bags behind the bounty hunter's cantle. As she reached his left boot, which was rammed into the stirrup, she stopped and looked up at him. She scratched her soft throat. 'Ya ain't dead is ya? It's hard to tell with some critters.'

'I ain't dead, Squirrel,' Iron Eyes whispered from lips which did not move.

She smiled, then tapped his leg. 'Then git down here and lend a gal a hand. I ain't feeding that nag of yours all on my lonesome.'

Iron Eyes remained with his hands on top of his saddle horn, staring straight ahead.

'Are ya listening to me?' she piped up. Then she clenched her fist and hit his leg even harder.

'I bin listening to ya all damn night, Squirrel,' he said with a sigh without looking down to where she was standing. 'My ears ache from listening to ya.'

A smile came over her face. 'I oughta shoot what's left of your stinking old carcass, Iron Eyes.'

He nodded. 'Looks like it's gonna be a nice day.'

The statement made her stop her pounding on his leg. She leaned to one side and stared hard at his scarred face. 'Did ya say it *looks* like?'

'Yep,' he replied.

She was not sure, but for the briefest of moments she thought she saw a tear in his nearer eye. 'Can ya see, Iron Eyes? Is them eyes of yours working again? Is they?'

His head turned and he looked down at her. For a moment he said nothing as he studied her. 'They sure are, Squirrel. Not perfect, but pretty good.'

She grabbed his leg. 'When did it happen?'

'I ain't sure,' he answered. 'It was when the sun hit me that I suddenly realized that I could see again. Must have bin slowly healing up all night but I never even noticed.'

Sally stepped back as the lean man eased himself off his saddle and swung his leg over the stallion's neck. He slid to the ground and stood beside her.

'Reckon ya ain't gonna be such a burden now.' She grinned.

Iron Eyes looked down at her. It was the first time he had been able to see every detail of her. He liked what he saw.

'You sure are pretty,' he said.

'And you are still the ugliest critter I ever done set eyes on, boy,' she responded, trying to hide her blushes from eyes which could now spot them.

'Yep.' He nodded in agreement. 'I sure am.'

127

The joyful female had moved towards the saddle-bags when she noticed her companion walking ahead into the churned-up ground. He was looking at it as if confused.

'What ya seen?' she called out.

Iron Eyes ran fingers through his limp hair and glanced at her. 'Which way you bin leading us?'

She pointed. 'Thataway. Where them cattle tracks are heading. Why?'

Iron Eyes rested his knuckles on his bony hips and looked in the opposite direction. For the first time for months his hunting instincts were working. Once again he seemed able, as of old, to read everything around him as clearly as if words were marked out in the sand. Slowly his left arm rose and a finger pointed.

'We oughta be heading thataway, Squirrel. That's why.'

'Are ya loco?' Sally ran to his side. 'The cattle tracks are heading east and you're pointing west.'

'It ain't the cattle tracks I'm looking at. Look at that sandy rise yonder. Shod tracks. Horse tracks.'

She looked and then saw the hoof marks of four riders cutting through the otherwise virgin sand. 'So a few horsemen rode over that rise. The steers tracks all head back there. Are we following the cattle or are we following riders?'

Iron Eyes gritted his teeth. 'We're trying to catch the varmints who killed ya folks. That's their tracks, Squirrel.'

128

Sally frowned. 'But them steers went over yonder.'

'Forget them.' The bounty hunter could feel his sight sharpening with every beat of his heart. 'The steers are long gone. Sold or butchered or both. The bastards who stole them and killed ya kinfolk went thataway after returning with their blood money.'

'Into the desert?'

'To El Remo.' Iron Eyes growled as if just saying the name of the infamous town was like sucking on rattler venom.

'What's El Remo?'

He rested his hand on her shoulder. 'Ya ever heard of Hell, Squirrel?'

She nodded. 'Sure I heard of Hell.'

'That's El Remo.' Iron Eyes spat and then dug two twisted cigars from his trail-coat pocket. He rammed one into her mouth and then gritted his teeth over the other. 'I trailed an *hombre* there once and had me a whole lot of lead to chew on by the time I managed to drag his dead carcass back over the border.'

'Ain't there no law there?' She pushed her hand into his pants pocket and fumbled around until she found a match. Her thumbnail struck it into flame and they both sucked smoke into their lungs.

'Nope,' the bounty hunter replied as smoke filtered through his teeth. 'Ain't no law there. Hell. Even the Devil rides shy of El Remo.'

She exhaled a line of smoke. 'Sounds dangerous.'

Iron Eyes sniffed the air and nodded his mane of

black hair. 'Can ya smell it?'

Sally took a deep breath and screwed up her pretty face. 'Damn right I can. What is that stink?'

'The stench of civilization, Squirrel.'

'I don't like it.'

'Me neither.'

She trailed him back to their animals and watched as he carefully and silently watered and grained both horse and burro.

'What we gonna do?' Sally asked him as she pondered the glowing tip of her cigar.

Chewing on his own smoke, Iron Eyes smiled. He straightened up and patted the gun grips jutting from his pants belt.

'We're gonna kill us some vermin, Squirrel.'

FIFTEEN

El Remo had only just come to grips with the fact that suddenly there was only one ruler within its aromatic purlieus. As human vultures stripped the bodies of the fallen clean of all their valuable possessions a new sickening stench filled its unruly streets. It was that of the rotting corpses piled high for all to see.

For all to take heed of and fear.

Mexican Pete had been quick to send Ty Harper and his newly hired gunmen to all corners of the town to gather in the rewards of his deadly takeover. Soon there would be another crimson warning to all those who might dare to stand up to the new ruler of El Remo in the future. Soon heads would be severed from dead men's necks and placed on pikes as warning to anyone who might challenge the bandit's authority.

Now as sunup spread its blistering heat across the lawless settlement the bandit with golden teeth thought he could relax and take stock.

Mexican Pete was wrong.

Even in a town where the Devil ruled there was a sense of trepidation filtering through the saloons and whorehouses. In spite of men's knowing that there was now only one gang and one supreme leader of that gang, doubts had already started to fester like open sores in the minds and hearts of those who now found they had a new boss to obey and pay.

Men who proclaim themselves top dog soon find there are many others who wish to usurp that position. Mexican Pete had unwittingly made himself a target. Others already knew it and the fact was slowly dawning on the bandit himself.

Wishing for a safer place from which to do business, Mexican Pete had moved from the cantina where he had secured victory over his rivals even before the gunsmoke had settled. He had travelled the length of El Remo to the large fortress-like building set on the very edge of the town. It was perched on the very edge of the cliff which overlooked the rugged drop down to the cave set amid a wall of boulders.

The best house in town had once belonged to Sven Anderson; he had ruled his section of El Remo from its imposing and solid structure. Like everything else in town the house now belonged to Mexican Pete.

For dead men do not require anywhere to reside. They become buzzard bait or even worse. As Mexican Pete stood on his veranda and cast his eyes down to the river far below he knew that Pedro and Sanchez were already chopping off the heads of all those who had once been his enemies. Soon the streets would be lined by those heads on pikes.

A sly grin etched his face.

Few men ever discover what it feels like to become a king but the bandit had done just that only hours earlier. Pete had at first liked the feeling, but now he was not so sure. The town had once had four men ruling everything. Now there was only him.

He had made himself a lone target.

Ty Harper made his way from the street, leaving through the unfamiliar building, a trail of dust behind him. He removed his Stetson and beat it against his leg.

'The boys are having themselves a mighty good time, Pete,' he told his leader as he rested a hip on the low wall which separated the rear of the building from a long drop.

'Cutting off heads is sort of fun.' Pete nodded.

'I got the rest of the boys to bring all the money they could find in Sumner's place here,' Harper told him. 'Must be at least twenty thousand in gold coin.'

Mexican Pete glanced at his top gun. 'What about Valez's place?'

'Even more.' Harper grinned. 'They're piling up

133

the boxes in the porch right now.'

Pete inhaled. 'I must have found that much in this house already and I haven't even been in all the rooms yet. This is very good, *amigo*.'

'Why don't ya get some shut-eye?' Harper suggested. 'Me and the boys can sort things out while ya rest.'

Pete gave a curious snort and rubbed his whiskered chin as though something he could not quite fathom was gnawing at his craw. 'I don't know, my friend. I have a bad feeling.'

'Like what?' Harper laughed and replaced his hat. 'Ya took over the whole town and had all ya enemies killed. What ya gotta worry about?'

'I'm not sure.' Mexican Pete shook his head thoughtfully.

'I've got it all under control, Pete,' Harper insisted.

Mexican Pete was walking back into the shade of the nearest room when he felt a shiver trace his spine, as though something had walked across his grave. He stopped and swallowed hard.

'What's wrong, Pete?' Harper asked. 'Ya look like ya seen a damn ghost.'

'Do ya believe in fate, *amigo*?' Pete asked. 'Some say that your entire life is mapped out. Even ya death is carved in stone and no man can alter that.'

Harper did not understand. 'What ya mean?'

Mexican Pete turned and looked straight into

Harper's eyes. He raised an eyebrow. He reached out, grabbed the man by the sleeve and drew him closer.

'Do ya think that a man such as me can see his future? Do ya, Ty? Do ya?'

'I heard tell of such things but. . . .'

'This is the best day of my life but something inside me is telling me to be careful.' The fearful words gushed from Pete's mouth. 'Something is telling me that I will not see the end of this day. Mexican Pete will not see sundown.'

'Ya just tuckered,' Harper said. 'It's bin a mighty busy couple of days for all of us.'

'*Sí, amigo.* You must be right.' Pete nodded. 'But I think that death is riding this way to visit with me.'

Harper smiled. 'Get some shut-eye.'

'I have drunk an ocean of liquor and yet I am not weary.' Pete said bluntly. 'Why am I not tired enough to close my eyes? Why do I see my own death each time I try?'

'I'll stand guard down here,' Harper told his boss. 'Ain't nobody gonna get to ya.'

'Be vigilant, *amigo.*' Mexican Pete continued walking into his newly acquired home but knew that even if he found the softest of beds he would not be able to sleep.

Death was riding towards El Remo.

Death thinly disguised as the deadly Iron Eyes.

*

135

The small burro was hauled to an abrupt stop as Sally stared down at the hooftracks left by the four horsemen in the sand. A sudden realization swept through her as her eyes focused upon one of the marks. Squirrel Sally felt her throat tighten. One of the hoofprints showed a distinctive split across its right side. Sally knew she had seen that very same shoemark before, back at her ranch.

'Look. Look,' Sally squeaked as her shaking finger pointed down at the churned-up sand.

Iron Eyes eased his stallion round and looked back at his companion. Her face was almost drained of colour. He tapped his spurs until the tall horse was standing next to its tiny cousin.

'What ya seen, Squirrel?' he asked.

'You was right. That track was left by one of the bastards who raided my ranch and killed my kin,' she blurted out.

Iron Eyes dismounted and knelt on the ground. He studied the tracks and knew exactly which one she meant. 'This'un with the split? Mighty peculiar-looking mark on that shoe. Oughta be dead easy for us to find that *hombre.*'

'Yep,' Sally answered excitedly. 'I seen that shoemark a whole heap of times around the ranch. I figured it must belong to one of the leaders of them vermin.'

The bounty hunter stood up again and looked at her. 'You're right, gal. When we find that horse we'll

136

find one of the killers. Maybe, like ya said, the leader of the pack.'

She nodded. 'Damn sure.'

Iron Eyes grabbed his horse's mane, threw his lean frame up on to his saddle, poked his boots into his stirrups and gathered up his reins. He steadied the powerful animal, then swung the stallion round until it was facing the direction in which the tracks were headed.

The place where the stench of El Remo was coming from.

His narrowed eyes bored out into the blistering heat. 'El Remo is just over the next rise, Squirrel.'

'I'm ready. Ready to kill, Iron Eyes.' Sally held her Winchester in her hands and gave a huge sigh.

He nodded.

'Let's go hunting.'

The merciless sun was at its highest as they entered the outskirts of El Remo. Every fibre of Iron Eyes's being had wanted to dig his sharp spurs into the flanks of his tall palomino stallion and ride with guns blazing into the stinking settlement, but he knew that the small burro could not keep pace. For the first time for months he had the taste of his prey drying the roof of his mouth. He knew that practically every living soul in the Mexican town was wanted dead or alive north of the unmarked border. It was an El Dorado for a bounty hunter, but Iron

Eyes realized that one mistake could bring a thousand or more guns raining down upon them.

Vermin like those in El Remo gathered together in lawless towns like this as if their combined numbers might somehow save them from their ultimate fate. For most it would; for those whom the infamous Iron Eyes hunted the story would have a different resolution.

Iron Eyes held his mighty horse in check, holding its reins to his chest. The animal, like its master, wanted to let loose and thunder through the dusty streets they had now entered.

The crumpled Wanted posters buried deep in his trail-coat pockets had not even been looked at since his sight had returned but the bounty hunter knew his memory was as good as anything printed on crude paper. His mind was filled with the faces and names of those he pursued. Even their individual quirks were branded into his emotionless brain.

It was high noon, although nobody in El Remo knew it. The blazing sun beat down across the town. There were no shadows except those directly beneath men and beasts.

An ice-cold fever washed over the faces of those who suddenly spotted the strange pair of riders as they made their way through the twisting streets deeper and deeper into the very heart of the dangerous town.

The young woman held her rifle in white-knuckled hands, with its wooden stock resting against her groin. Sally kept her index finger curled around its trigger in readiness. Yet it was not the little figure dressed in the undertaker's over-sized frock-coat that made the onlookers anxious. It was the sight of her emaciated companion.

Iron Eyes had become legendary on both sides of the border. His reputation and description always rode before him, chilling the hearts of those who knew that when it came to bounty hunters there was only one who should be truly feared.

Iron Eyes.

No other of his deadly profession would have dared to enter El Remo. His long black hair hung limply across his broad shoulders as he held the reins in one hand whilst keeping the fingers of the other a few inches away from the grips of his infamous Navy Colts.

People began to run away. Everyone headed in the same direction. Iron Eyes remained stone-faced as he teased his horse on with jabs of his bloodstained spurs.

'Where we heading, Iron Eyes?' Sally asked.

'The same place that all them yella bellies are running, Squirrel gal,' Iron Eyes replied without moving a muscle. 'They seem to be real eager to tell someone about us. Reckon that someone might be one of the varmints we're hunting.'

'I'm ready to kill,' Sally averred.

139

'Be lean with ya ammo, Squirrel,' the high rider warned his companion. 'I got me a feeling that we'll need every last bullet we got between us before this is over.'

'I'll not waste lead,' she reassured him.

Before Iron Eyes and Squirrel Sally had reached the heart of the town they had passed some of the severed heads of those who had fallen victim to Mexican Pete's henchmen. At least a dozen heads were glaring down with dead eyes from the swaying pike staffs that lined both sides of the long, twisting thoroughfare.

It was a hideous sight that neither the bounty hunter nor the young Sally had expected. They had no idea of what had occurred the previous night. All they could do was remain stone-faced as they guided their walking mounts around the decapitated bodies, towards the very centre of El Remo.

Years of experience told Iron Eyes that if you wanted to find your prey you came to the very middle of a town and found the largest and busiest of its drinking holes. This would be where the liquor flowed more freely. Where tongues loosened as the fiery alcohol blurred men's and women's minds.

Without saying a word to Sally the bounty hunter had been studying the ground across which they were guiding their mounts. They had barely gone 200 yards into El Remo before his bullet-coloured pupils again recognized the hoof-tracks that led them here: the horseshoe mark with the split across it. Iron Eyes looked up and saw the horse that had left that unmistakable mark in the sand. It was still tied to the hitching pole outside the cantina.

Iron Eyes turned the tall stallion and it paced up to the hitching pole next to the dapple grey. His attention was drawn to the dried blood which covered each of the steps down from the building's boardwalk. The sand was scarlet all around his snorting horse. Blood took a long time to go away in a climate where rain was as rare as rooster teeth.

Many curious eyes watched them as Sally reined in beside her companion. She dropped to the ground and cranked the mechanism of her carbine. The sound seemed to echo all about them. The young woman tied her reins to the latigo of the horse's saddle.

'Kinda interested in us,' Sally observed, glancing up to the man who was watching all those who watched them.

'Yep. They sure are.' Iron Eyes slid down from his high perch. Dust eddied around his boots as he rested both hands on his gun grips. Every eye was upon them. 'We sure have bitten us off a real big chunk of trouble here, gal. Don't be feared, though.'

'I ain't feared.' Sally watched as the skeletal figure secured his reins, then reached down and grabbed hold of the grey horse's leg. He pulled it up and satisfied himself that this was the animal they had been

141

tracking for so many hours.

'I figured as much,' he drawled.

'That the nag?' Sally asked.

'Yep.' Iron Eyes released his grip and the horse slowly lowered its leg until its hoof was on the sand. 'Now all we gotta do is find the owner of that horse.'

'Say. Why'd ya figure all them damn heads have bin stuck on them poles, Iron Eyes?' Squirrel Sally was beginning to wonder whether that was the fate that awaited all folks who dared enter this lawless town.

'Damned if I know,' Iron Eyes answered honestly. 'Damned if I care.'

He placed a boot on to the steps and started to walk up the short flight. The sound of his spurs seemed to send most of the curious on their way. By the time he and Sally had reached the boardwalk there was no one outside the cantina. Again Iron Eyes paused as he found a long thin black cigar in his pocket. He snapped it in two. His bony fingers rammed one half between the woman's awaiting lips before he raised his half to his own. He gripped the weed, then found a match in his pants pocket. A thumbnail struck the match into flame and he offered it to Sally to light her cigar before he filled his own lungs with the strong smoke. He shook the match and tossed it aside.

'Ya figure he's in here?' Sally asked as she vainly tried to look over the swing doors.

'For all we know one of them heads stuck on them poles might belong to him, gal.' The bounty hunter sighed as his teeth gripped the smoking cigar firmly. 'I sure hope not though. I'm kinda hankering for a fight.'

'We gonna go in this saloon, Iron Eyes?' she asked, adjusting the sleeves on her coat, though her finger remained on the rifle's trigger. 'I ain't never bin in a saloon before.'

He did not reply. Satisfied that there were no guns ready to backshoot either of them Iron Eyes turned, placed a hand on the swing doors and walked into the cantina with her at his side. It was as if the sound of his spurs had sent most of the cantina's patrons fleeing out through the back way. There were only a score of men remaining at the tables as the bounty hunter strode towards the wet counter and the terrified-looking barkeep.

'Whiskey,' Iron Eyes demanded through a cloud of smoke.

'Whiskey it is.' The man behind the counter had turned to reach for a bottle from a shelf when he felt the cold steel barrel of the bounty hunters Navy Colt against his sweating neck.

'Who owns that dapple grey out yonder?' Iron Eyes muttered in a low whisper.

The man swallowed hard. 'Dapple grey?'

'Yep.'

'That belongs to Mexican Pete,' the trembling

143

barkeep managed to reply as he turned back to face his horrific interrogator.

Iron Eyes pushed his gun back into his belt beside its twin and nodded thoughtfully. 'Mexican Pete. Got himself a mouthful of gold teeth, if I recollect.'

'That's him.' The barkeep gulped. 'Him and his boys done took over the whole town last night. Slaughtered every other gang member in El Remo. That's why them heads are being put on top of them stakes. One of his boys known as One-eared Sanchez has bin real busy all morning with his machete.'

'Mexican Pete is worth a tidy sum in Texas,' the bounty hunter remarked. 'Dead or alive.'

'Dead or alive?' The barkeep was now shaking so badly he had to rest both hands on top of the counter to stop himself from falling over. 'Y-ya ain't a lawman, are ya? This ain't a real healthy place for lawmen.'

'Nope. I ain't no lawman.' Iron Eyes sucked in smoke and then let it to filter through his teeth. 'I'm worse.'

'Worse?'

'I'm Iron Eyes.'

Suddenly the batwings swung violently open and One-eared Sanchez led five dust-caked gunmen into the cantina. The sound of the swing doors rocking on their hinges drew the attention of everyone in the cantina.

The machete hung low in the bandit's left hand as

he rested the palm of the other on his holstered Remington. The men who flanked Sanchez held their rifles and six-shooters in readiness as Pedro joined the group. Every man who stood with the noonday sun on their back had found what they had all been seeking.

Iron Eyes.

Sanchez raised his brutal machete and waved it at the tall bounty hunter, who instinctively pushed the small woman behind the tails of his long trail coat.

'I know you,' Sanchez snarled in anger. 'You are the gringo called Iron Eyes. You are a stinking bounty hunter.'

Iron Eyes gave a slow nod and a cruel grin. 'And by the looks of it I'd wager that you are the snot-sucking One-eared Sanchez.'

Pedro shuffled between the other gunmen and came to stand next to Sanchez. 'Let us go and tell Pete.'

'Silence,' Sanchez roared. 'I have been insulted by a very ugly Apache. I have to kill him for this. I do not like stinking Apaches. Die, Iron Eyes.'

The bandit leaned back and threw the savage blade at the bounty hunter. Iron Eyes leaned to the side as the machete embedded itself in the wall beside him.

Without warning Iron Eyes drew, cocked and fired his Navy Colts in rapid succession. Flames of fury went blistering through the dusty air like rods of lightning. Stunned customers threw themselves on to the floor in all directions.

One-eared Sanchez was hit high and he fell. Two of the other men buckled and died before they had even managed to squeeze their triggers.

Bullets were returned in equal ferocity from the hired gunmen who had survived the first volley. But their lives were also on the brink of ending.

The cantina rocked as the deafening noise grew and grew as thumbs dragged hammers and fingers eased triggers back.

A terrified Pedro ran out through the choking gunsmoke and dragged the reins of the dapple grey free of the hitching rail. He mounted, spurred and went galloping along the street in the direction of the large house where his leader was holed up.

Like a creature from another world Iron Eyes moved through the smoke with his guns gripped firmly in his hands. His eyes darted from one body to the next until he was sure that they were all dead.

He returned to the bar. 'Whiskey.'

With a trembling hand the barkeep placed a bottle on the counter.

'Ya sure done for them,' the frightened man said. 'Ya seemed to get angry awful fast.'

Iron Eyes shook the spent casing from his guns and dug into his trail coat pocket for fresh bullets. 'Always get ornery when some critter calls me an Injun. I sure hates Injuns.'

Sally was still standing where her tall champion had pushed her into the corner where the counter met the wall. The bloody machete, was a mere six inches above her head and still quivering.

'Ya sure are fast, Iron Eyes.' She gulped and the cigar fell from her lips. 'I didn't even have me time to fire my rifle once.'

Iron Eyes had reloaded both his guns and pushed them back into his belt. He clawed two glasses along the bar top and filled them both. He handed one to her, then tossed the contents of the other into his mouth and swallowed. The bounty hunter pointed at Sanchez.

'That's one of the varmints that killed ya folks, Squirrel.'

'How'd ya know?' she asked, taking a sip of the whiskey.

'He always rides with Mexican Pete, gal.' Iron Eyes tossed another shot of whiskey into his mouth and savoured it before swallowing. 'C'mon. We got to finish the job now.'

'Where we going?' Sally asked.

'After Pedro,' Iron Eyes answered faster than he had drawn his weapons a moment earlier. 'He's high-tailed it to tell Pete that I'm after him.'

'But where is this Mexican Pete?' Sally managed to finish her drink and coughed.

The barkeep leaned over the counter and tapped the side of his own nose. 'If'n ya looking to find

147

Mexican Pete and the rest of his bunch, head on down to the real big house perched on the cliff.'

Iron Eyes pushed the bottle back towards the man. 'Hold on to this till I get back.'

The man nodded.

'C'mon, Squirrel.' The tall bounty hunter turned and headed back towards the swing doors with Sally on his tail.

SIXTEEN

The dread which had haunted Mexican Pete ever since he had taken over El Remo suddenly found a focus. Pedro left the dapple grey hitched to a rail outside the large house and ran yelling in terror through the vast interior. Ty Harper dragged the bandit to the balcony and slapped the hysterical man until he was able to speak clearly.

'What in tarnation is wrong with ya?'

'Iron Eyes.' Pedro spewed the name and pointed in the direction of the town. 'He is here. He is killing our men, *amigo*. He is a monster.'

Harper released his hold on the quivering bandit. He was about to speak when he saw an ashen-faced Mexican Pete emerge from a room at the rear of the great house.

'Iron Eyes?' Pete repeated the name. 'Here?'

Pedro dropped to his knees and clasped his hands together as though in prayer. '*Sí*, Pete. The man who

149

is a ghost. He has come and he is killing our men in the cantina.'

Mexican Pete hauled the bandit off his knees and shook him violently. 'The bounty hunter has come here?'

'*Sí, amigo.*' Pedro sobbed. 'He has killed Sanchez. He has killed them all by now.'

Horror was carved into the face of the bandit leader as he paced to the balcony and stared down over its low balustrade at the cliff where he knew the cave was situated. He rubbed his neck and then glanced at Harper.

'Iron Eyes,' he said. 'I have seen this creature before. He is not like other men. He cannot be killed. Bullets pass through him and he does not die.'

Harper shook his head. 'Ya need sleep, Pete. Ya talking plumb loco. All men can be killed.'

Mexican Pete was breathing fast. 'Not this man. If he is a man. I tell ya, we are in trouble. Like I said before, I had a dream. A nightmare. It has come to pass. Iron Eyes is death.'

Harper gritted his teeth and checked both his guns before turning to Pedro. 'Go see how many of our men are in the house, Pedro. Round them all up and bring them here.'

Pedro gave a terrified nod and ran.

Harper had always admired Mexican Pete. Admired and feared the man who, he knew, was probably one of the most dangerous bandits he had ever ridden with. But now all he could see was a man who was floundering in irrational madness.

'One man can't take us all on.' Harper tried to reassure the shaken man.

Mexican Pete kept looking to where the cave was just visible from where he was standing. 'Iron Eyes is not a real man, Ty. I have told ya. He ain't. Ya can't kill a phantom. It's like trying to shoot down a cloud. Can't be done.'

'Ya sound scared, Pete,' Harper said. 'I ain't never seen Mexican Pete scared of nothing or nobody before.'

Mexican Pete raised himself up and turned as Pedro came back to the balcony. He was alone.

'Where's the rest of the boys, Pedro?' Harper snarled. 'I told ya to bring them here.'

Pedro shrugged. 'I find no one. I checked the stables and all their horses are gone. There is no one here but us three.'

Mexican Pete sighed heavily. It was the sigh of a man who was seeing his darkest visions taking shape around him. 'Three men against Iron Eyes? We are dead men.'

Harper refused to be beaten. 'C'mon, Pedro. We'll give that Iron Eyes a welcome he ain't ever gonna forget.'

The bandit leader remained where he was and watched the last two of his men marching back through the vast house towards the front entrance.

'Fools,' Pete whispered. 'You cannot kill those who are already dead.'

Both men reached the wide-open front door and drew their weaponry. They stared out into the street. It was virtually empty. Only dust blew across its length. Clouds of dust whipped up from the cliff behind them.

Pedro crouched next to the doorframe and tried to hold on to both his guns as his entire body shook with fear. He wanted to speak but then he saw something out beyond the clouds of billowing dust. It was the bounty hunter he had seen dispatch Sanchez. It was Iron Eyes.

'Is that him, Pedro?' Ty Harper leaned on the opposite side of the doorframe and raised his guns to hip height as he too caught fleeting glimpses of the terrifying man who was walking down the centre of the street towards them. 'Is that him? Is that Iron Eyes?'

Pedro could only nod.

'He gotta be loco,' Harper surmised. 'Walking straight into our guns like that. Don't he have no brains at all?'

The smaller bandit got back to his feet. He was almost whimpering. 'Pete said he is not a real man. Look. He comes to kill us all, *amigo*. I am going.'

With a gun in each hand Harper was unable to grab hold of his fleeing *compadre*. He snarled and watched as the panicked Pedro raced out to the awaiting dapple grey, tore its reins free of a hitching rail and mounted.

There came a sound like thunder.

Suddenly the bandit was standing in his stirrups. His entire body went crimson as chunks of flesh were ripped from him by the bullets tearing through him.

Harper watched Pedro's lifeless body fall from the horse and crash to the ground. He clutched his guns and squeezed their triggers. His bullets cut into the cloud of dust. Then, as it cleared, he saw nothing but an empty street.

'He's gone,' Harper huffed angrily. 'Where'd he go?'

'Here.' The whispering voice came from just beyond the door.

Harper swung on his heels and cocked his hammers but it was too late. Iron Eyes blasted both his Navy Colts straight into the outlaw's midriff. Blood sprayed from the back of Harper's vest and covered the whitewashed wall. His guns fell from his hands as he slid down to the floor. A pool of blood spread out around the dead outlaw.

'C'mon, Squirrel.' Iron Eyes beckoned to his small companion as he stepped over the dead man and peered through the house towards the sun-baked balcony. Clutching her Winchester she followed.

The sound of Iron Eyes's spurs echoed inside the interior of the house as his spare figure led the way to where he could smell his prey.

Sally clung on to her rifle and shuffled along behind him. The tiled floor felt like ice to her bare feet. She wanted to speak but had no words. No words which made sense of what she was witnessing. The tall man with the smoking Navy Colts in his bony hands was unlike any other person she had ever encountered.

He seemed actually to be able to follow the scent of the man he was hunting.

They reached the balcony but there was no one there.

'He's high-tailed it.' Sally frowned.

Iron Eyes closed his eyes and took a deep breath. He strode to the very edge of the balcony, leaned on the low tiled wall and gazed over it. He stared down and just caught sight of Mexican Pete disappearing into the cave. The perilous descent had proved less frightening than facing the bounty hunter.

'The coward went down there, Squirrel.' Iron Eyes removed the spent casings from his guns and replaced them with fresh bullets from his deep coat pockets. 'I'm going down there after the varmint.'

Sally leaned over and stared at the steep drop. 'Ya don't have to risk ya life just to avenge my folks for me, Iron Eyes.'

'I ain't.' Iron Eyes dropped both guns into his trail-coat pockets and looped his long thin legs over the wall. 'I'm hunting him for his reward money, gal.'

'What?'

154

'Mexican Pete is worth one thousand dollars.' Iron Eyes winked and started to make his way down the sheer drop. 'That's an awful lot of whiskey and cigars.'

She removed her ill-fitting coat, tucked her rifle under her arm and clambered over the wall to stand beside him. 'Then I'm coming as well.'

'Why?'

'I want me a share of that money.' Sally nodded. 'Buy me a new pipe with that kinda money.'

'Reckon ya are a full-grown woman after all, Squirrel,' Iron Eyes observed.

Both of them clambered down the side of the cliff. The boulders were a lot bigger close up than they had appeared from the balcony and this enabled them to make good time to the entrance of the cave. They rested for a few moments as Iron Eyes stared at the gaping hole in the side of the cliff face.

'What we gonna do?' asked Sally, resting her head against his elbow as she tried to look inside the cave. She aimed the long barrel of her Winchester into the darkness. 'Let me fire a few rounds in there. I might get lucky and hit the bastard.'

The bounty hunter pushed her back. 'Ya want to have ya head blown off, gal? You stay here. If Pete comes back out then ya can shoot him. Savvy?'

Sally frowned and slapped his arm. 'Ya worse than an old woman.'

Suddenly a voice came from the cave. 'You will

never get me, Iron Eyes. I ain't ready to die.'

Iron Eyes pulled one of his guns from his pocket and drew its hammer back until it locked fully into position. He held the weapon against his chest, inhaled deeply, then threw himself into the cave entrance. Iron Eyes landed on the hard rocky surface just as a shot came from deep inside the belly of the cave. It passed within inches of the bounty hunter.

'Ya missed me, Pete.' Iron Eyes stretched out his arm and trained the long seven-inch barrel on the darkness ahead of him. 'You might not be ready to die but I'm sure ready to kill ya though, Pete.'

Another shot lit up the cave tunnel. Iron Eyes felt the heat of the bullet as it passed over his head. He squeezed his own trigger. The brief flash of the bullet as it left the barrel of Iron Eyes's gun was enough for the bounty hunter to see his elusive prey. He dragged the hammer back again and fired once more.

This time he saw Mexican Pete knocked back-wards by the impact of the deadly accurate shot. The deafening reverberations slowly evaporated as Iron Eyes got back to his feet.

'I told ya it was your time to die, Pete,' the thin figure drawled. He struck a match and stared at the dead man in its flickering flame.

Sally looked around the cave wall. She fired her rifle. Her bullet hit the bandit dead centre, a mere inch away from the hole left by the bounty hunter's bullet.

Iron Eyes blew the match out and turned to her.
'Feel better, Squirrel?'

She began to cry.

FINALE

The stagecoach the bounty hunter had found abandoned behind the cantina was full of dead wanted men. Men who, Iron Eyes knew, were wanted dead or alive across the border. He closed the door after placing Mexican Pete's body on the top of the valuable pile of corpses. He ran a match down the side of the carriage door and cupped its flame in his hands. He lit a cigar, sucked in the smoke, then tossed the match aside.

Sally had tied both the palomino stallion and the small burro to the stagecoach's tailgate. She moved to the side of her tall companion and then forced her small hand down into his pants pocket. Her fingers moved around in search of something.

Iron Eyes grabbed hold of her wrist and pulled it back out.

'What ya looking for, Squirrel?' he asked through a cloud of cigar smoke.

158

'A match,' she replied, fluttering her eyelashes.

He pulled the cigar from his mouth, pushed it between her lips and bent over, 'Wrong pocket.'

Sally puffed away, then climbed up the side of the coach like a cat until she reached the high seat. 'Found me something in that pocket of yours a whole heap more interesting than a match though. Mighty interesting.'

'You trouble me, Squirrel gal.' Iron Eyes raised a leg, placed it on the front wheel of the coach and hoisted himself up the side of the vehicle until he also reached the driver's seat.

She giggled as she watched him nervously unwrapping the hefty reins from around the brake pole. When they were free he held them firmly in his hands.

'We gonna get hitched?' she asked as she sucked on the cigar.

Iron Eyes looked at her. 'You trouble me a whole lot, gal.'

'Where we headed?' Sally asked.

'Cooperville,' Iron Eyes replied.

'I think ya love me.'

'Will ya get it into ya head? I don't love ya.' Iron Eyes slapped the reins across the backs of the team and started the stagecoach on its way. Then her agile fingers slid into his pants pocket again.

The six-horse team pulled its heavy cargo away from the front of the cantina as its driver vainly tried

159

to control not only them but the female beside him. Fidgeting like someone with ants in his pants, Iron Eyes protested.

'Will ya quit doing that? I told ya I ain't got no matches in that pocket, Squirrel.'

She kept her hand in his pocket and laughed.

'Are ya deaf?' Iron Eyes tried to wriggle away but there was no place to go. 'I ain't got no matches in—'

'I ain't looking for matches, ya dumb ugly fool.' Sally roared with laughter as the stagecoach headed out of El Remo on its way back to the border and a town where Iron Eyes knew he would be able to lay claim to the reward money on all the dead bodies piled high inside the vehicle.

She moved closer to him.

'And I ain't in love with ya neither.' Iron Eyes whipped the reins down hard across the backs of the horses, encouraging the team to gather even more pace.

It was a long way to Cooperville.

An awful long way.